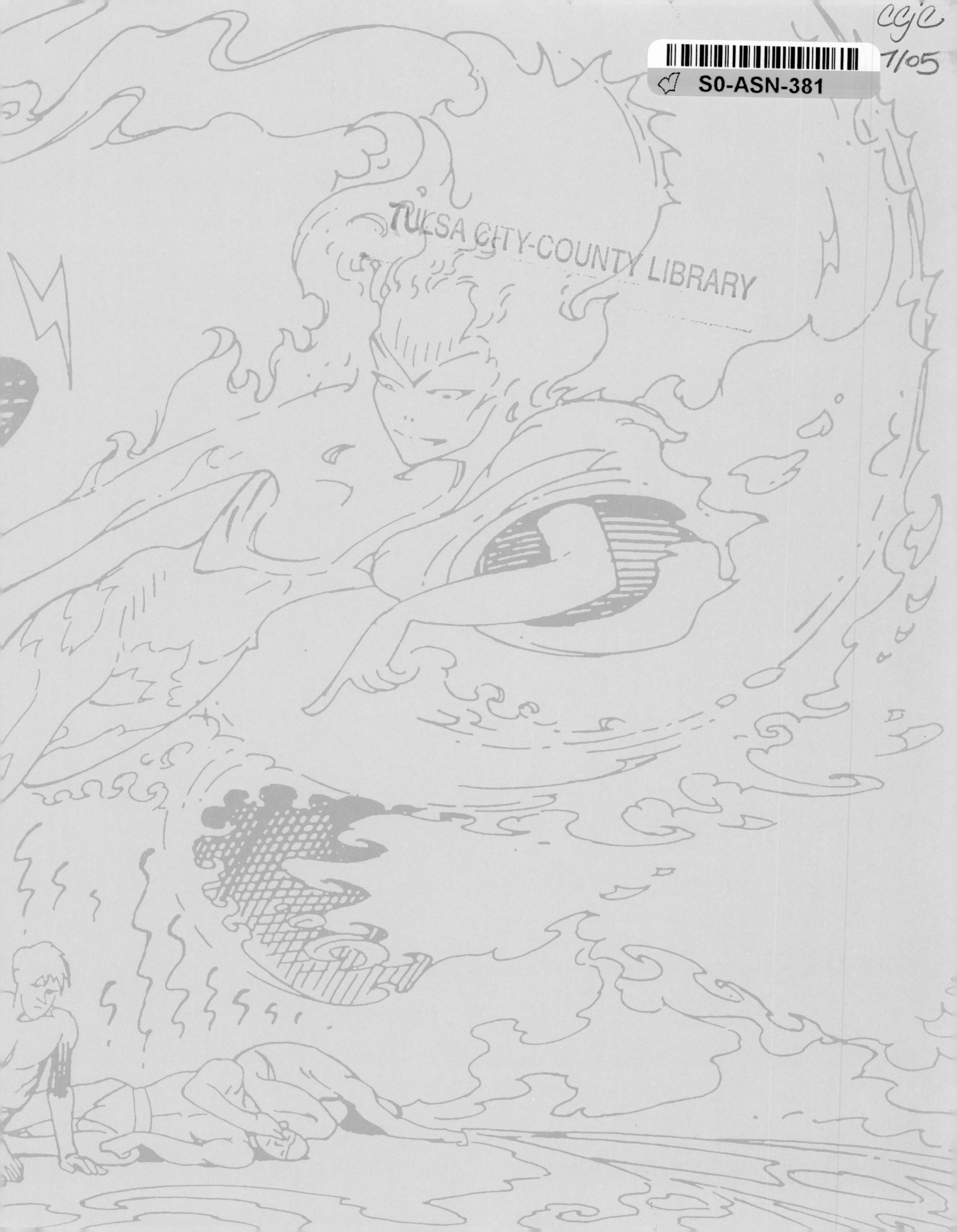

FAIRY TALES OF OSCAR WILDE

ILLUSTRATED ★ BY

P. CRAIG RUSSELL

THE YOUNG KING
THE REMARKABLE ROCKET

NANTIER · BEALL · MINOUSTCHINE
Publishing inc.
new york

Also available:

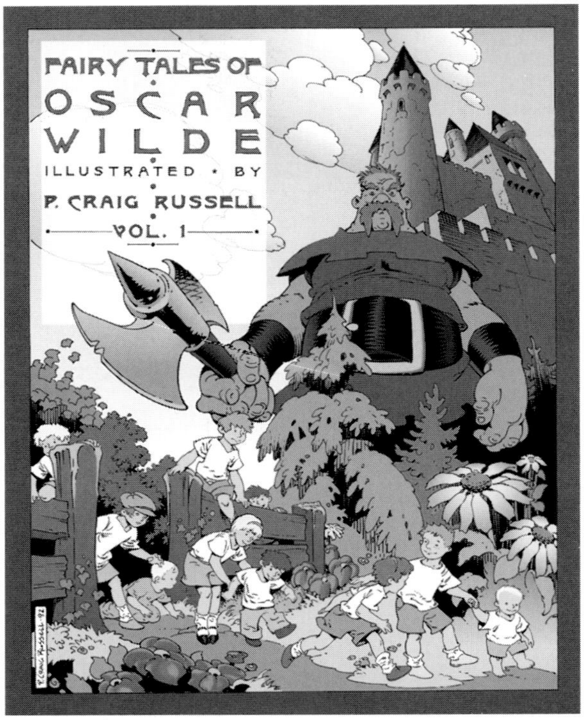
FAIRY TALES OF
OSCAR
WILDE
ILLUSTRATED • BY
P. CRAIG RUSSELL
VOL. 1

$15.95 (+$2 P&H)
Including
The Selfish Giant
The Star Child

ISBN 1-56163-085-3
Lettering by Michael Taylor
Colors by Digital Chameleon

2 3 4 5 6 7 8 9

Send for our complete
catalog of graphic albums:
NBM Publishing Inc.
185 Madison Ave., Suite 1504
New York, NY 10016

Printed in Hong Kong

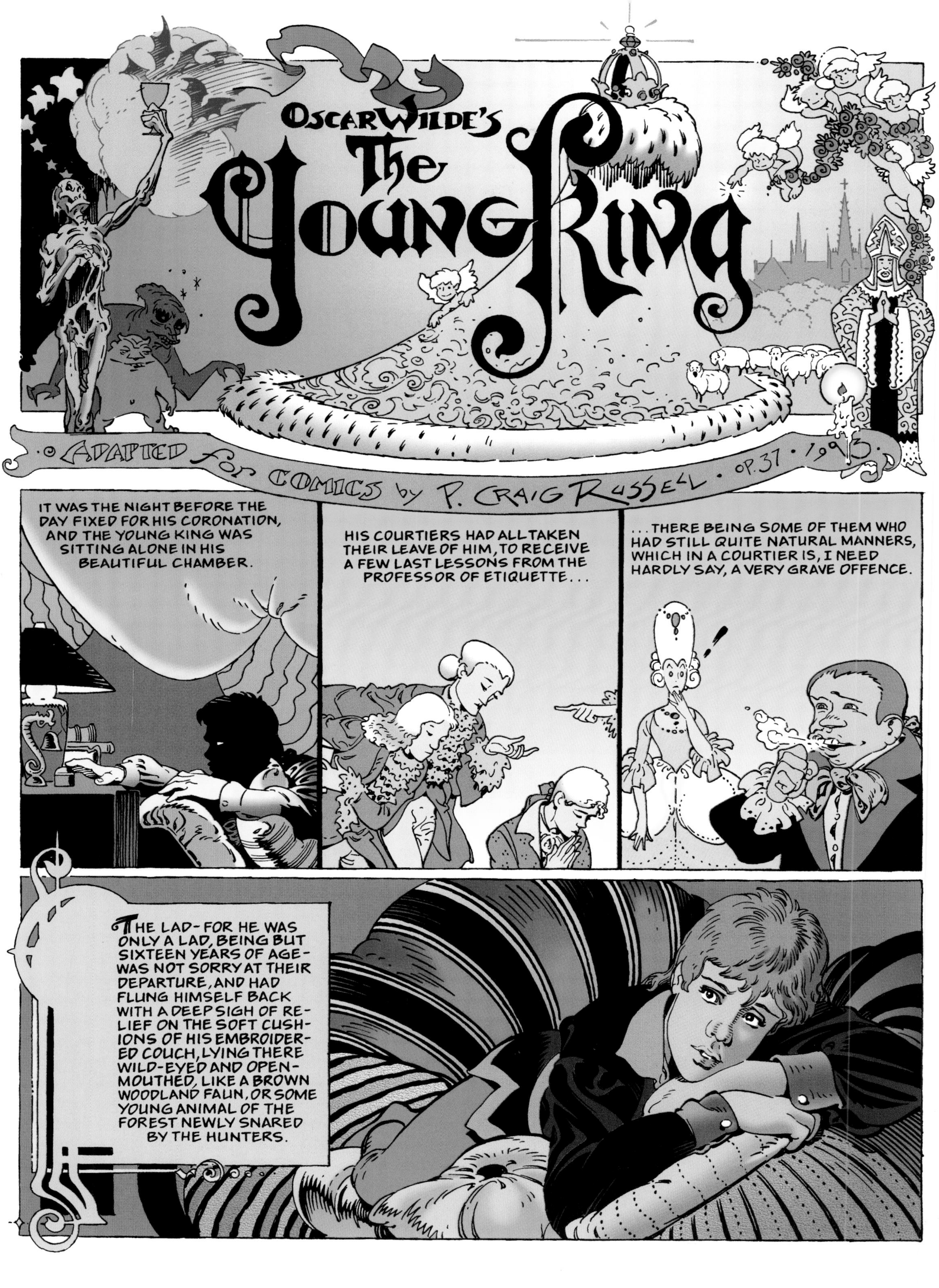
OSCAR WILDE'S
THE YOUNG KING
ADAPTED FOR COMICS BY P. CRAIG RUSSELL · OP. 37 · 1993 ·
IT WAS THE NIGHT BEFORE THE DAY FIXED FOR HIS CORONATION, AND THE YOUNG KING WAS SITTING ALONE IN HIS BEAUTIFUL CHAMBER.
HIS COURTIERS HAD ALL TAKEN THEIR LEAVE OF HIM, TO RECEIVE A FEW LAST LESSONS FROM THE PROFESSOR OF ETIQUETTE . . .
. . . THERE BEING SOME OF THEM WHO HAD STILL QUITE NATURAL MANNERS, WHICH IN A COURTIER IS, I NEED HARDLY SAY, A VERY GRAVE OFFENCE.
!
THE LAD- FOR HE WAS ONLY A LAD, BEING BUT SIXTEEN YEARS OF AGE- WAS NOT SORRY AT THEIR DEPARTURE, AND HAD FLUNG HIMSELF BACK WITH A DEEP SIGH OF RELIEF ON THE SOFT CUSHIONS OF HIS EMBROIDERED COUCH, LYING THERE WILD-EYED AND OPEN-MOUTHED, LIKE A BROWN WOODLAND FAUN, OR SOME YOUNG ANIMAL OF THE FOREST NEWLY SNARED BY THE HUNTERS.

AND, INDEED, IT WAS THE HUNTERS WHO HAD FOUND HIM, COMING UPON HIM ALMOST BY CHANCE AS, BARE-LIMBED AND PIPE IN HAND, HE WAS FOLLOWING THE FLOCK OF THE POOR GOATHERD WHO HAD BROUGHT HIM UP, AND WHOSE SON HE HAD ALWAYS FANCIED HIMSELF TO BE.

THE CHILD OF THE OLD KING'S ONLY DAUGHTER BY A SECRET MARRIAGE WITH ONE MUCH BENEATH HER IN STATION...

HE HAD BEEN, WHEN BUT A WEEK OLD, STOLEN FROM HIS MOTHER'S SIDE AS SHE SLEPT AND GIVEN TO AN OLD PEASANT AND HIS WIFE WHO LIVED IN A REMOTE PART OF THE FOREST.

GRIEF, OR AS SOME SUGGESTED, A SWIFT ITALIAN POISON IN A CUP OF SPICED WINE, SLEW WITHIN AN HOUR OF HER WAKENING THE GIRL WHO HAD GIVEN HIM BIRTH...

...AND AS THE TRUSTY MESSENGER WHO BARE THE CHILD ACROSS THE SADDLE-BOW STOOPED FROM HIS WEARY HORSE AND KNOCKED AT THE RUDE DOOR OF THE GOATHERD'S HUT...

...THE BODY OF THE PRINCESS WAS BEING LOWERED INTO AN OPEN GRAVE IN A DESERTED CHURCHYARD BEYOND THE CITY GATES.

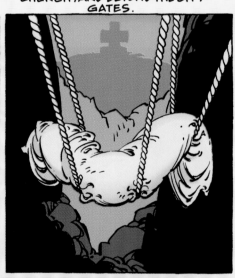

...A GRAVE WHERE IT WAS SAID THAT ANOTHER BODY WAS ALSO LYING, THAT OF A YOUNG MAN OF MARVELLOUS AND FOREIGN BEAUTY, WHOSE HANDS WERE TIED BEHIND HIM WITH A KNOTTED CORD, AND WHOSE BREAST WAS STABBED WITH MANY RED WOUNDS.

SUCH, AT LEAST, WAS THE STORY THAT MEN WHISPERED TO EACH OTHER.

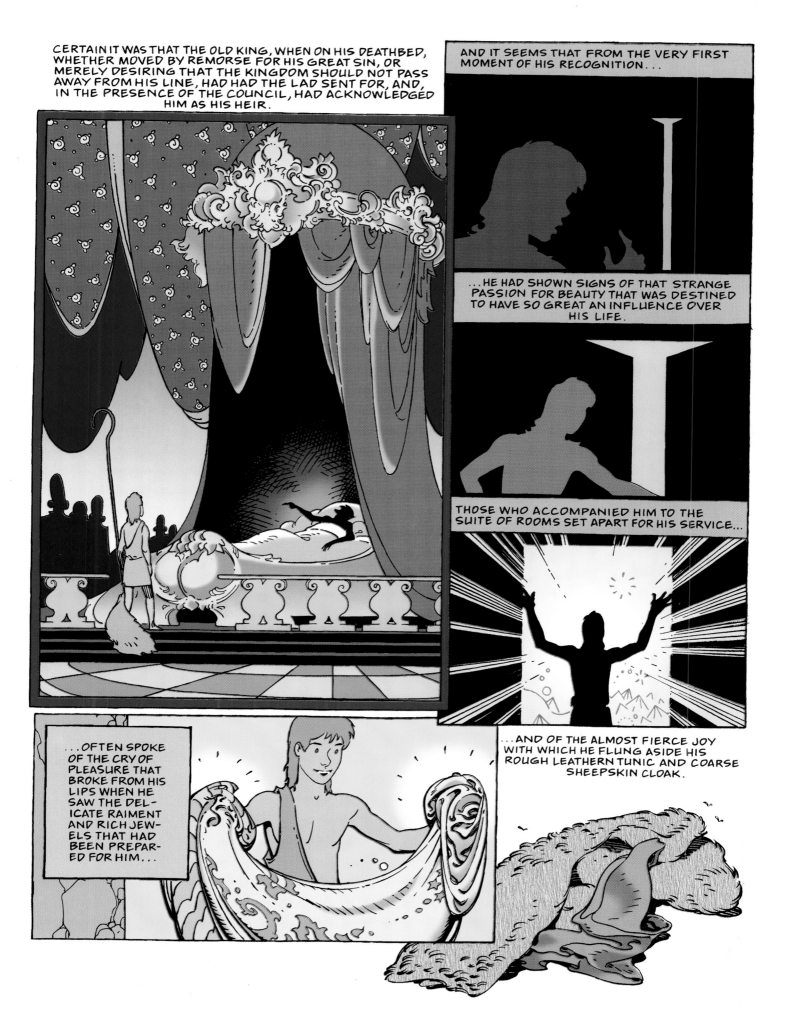

CERTAIN IT WAS THAT THE OLD KING, WHEN ON HIS DEATHBED, WHETHER MOVED BY REMORSE FOR HIS GREAT SIN, OR MERELY DESIRING THAT THE KINGDOM SHOULD NOT PASS AWAY FROM HIS LINE, HAD HAD THE LAD SENT FOR, AND, IN THE PRESENCE OF THE COUNCIL, HAD ACKNOWLEDGED HIM AS HIS HEIR.

AND IT SEEMS THAT FROM THE VERY FIRST MOMENT OF HIS RECOGNITION...

...HE HAD SHOWN SIGNS OF THAT STRANGE PASSION FOR BEAUTY THAT WAS DESTINED TO HAVE SO GREAT AN INFLUENCE OVER HIS LIFE.

THOSE WHO ACCOMPANIED HIM TO THE SUITE OF ROOMS SET APART FOR HIS SERVICE...

...OFTEN SPOKE OF THE CRY OF PLEASURE THAT BROKE FROM HIS LIPS WHEN HE SAW THE DELICATE RAIMENT AND RICH JEWELS THAT HAD BEEN PREPARED FOR HIM...

...AND OF THE ALMOST FIERCE JOY WITH WHICH HE FLUNG ASIDE HIS ROUGH LEATHERN TUNIC AND COARSE SHEEPSKIN CLOAK.

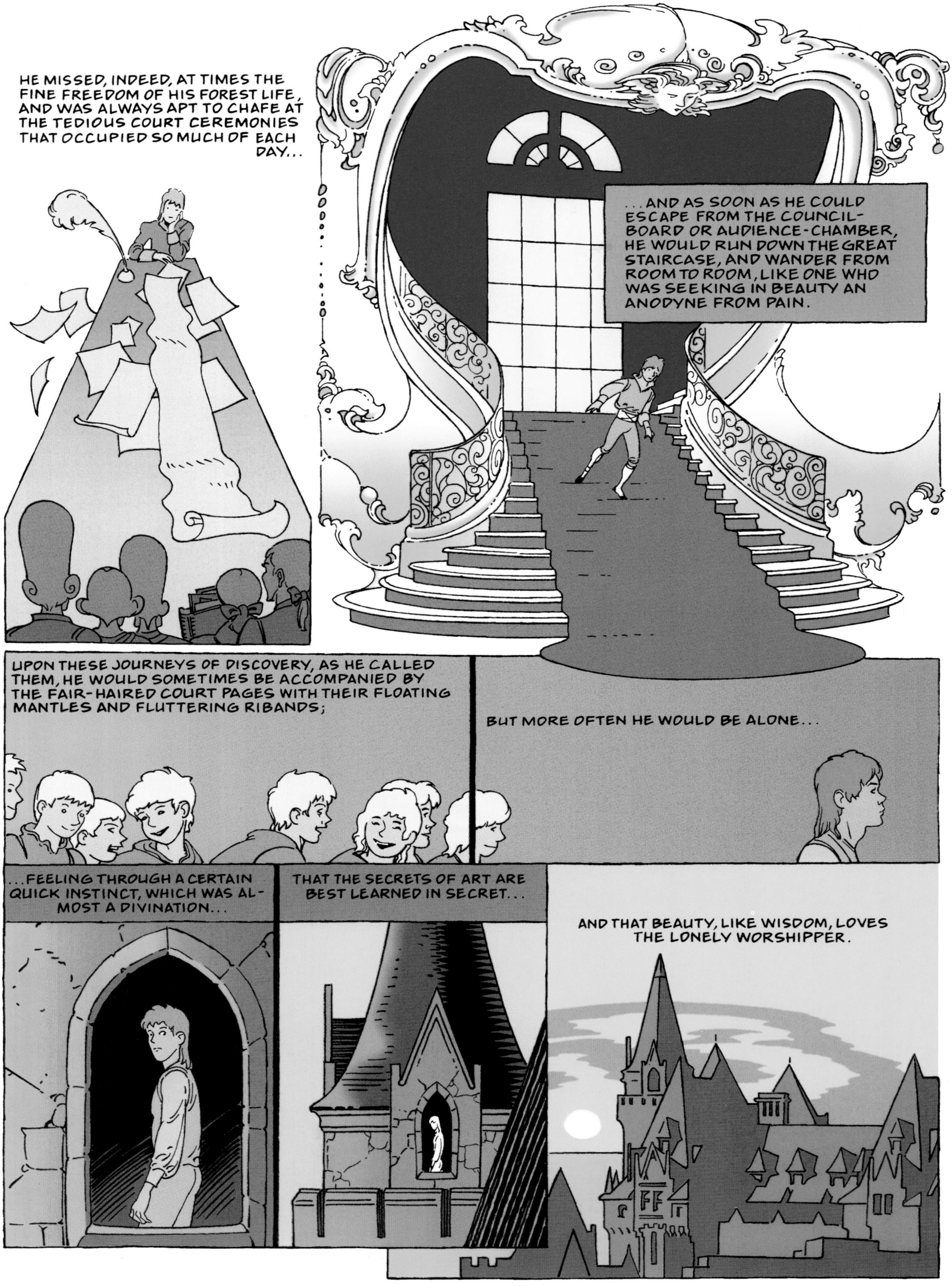
HE MISSED, INDEED, AT TIMES THE FINE FREEDOM OF HIS FOREST LIFE, AND WAS ALWAYS APT TO CHAFE AT THE TEDIOUS COURT CEREMONIES THAT OCCUPIED SO MUCH OF EACH DAY...
...AND AS SOON AS HE COULD ESCAPE FROM THE COUNCIL-BOARD OR AUDIENCE-CHAMBER, HE WOULD RUN DOWN THE GREAT STAIRCASE, AND WANDER FROM ROOM TO ROOM, LIKE ONE WHO WAS SEEKING IN BEAUTY AN ANODYNE FROM PAIN.
UPON THESE JOURNEYS OF DISCOVERY, AS HE CALLED THEM, HE WOULD SOMETIMES BE ACCOMPANIED BY THE FAIR-HAIRED COURT PAGES WITH THEIR FLOATING MANTLES AND FLUTTERING RIBANDS;
BUT MORE OFTEN HE WOULD BE ALONE...
...FEELING THROUGH A CERTAIN QUICK INSTINCT, WHICH WAS ALMOST A DIVINATION...
THAT THE SECRETS OF ART ARE BEST LEARNED IN SECRET...
AND THAT BEAUTY, LIKE WISDOM, LOVES THE LONELY WORSHIPPER.

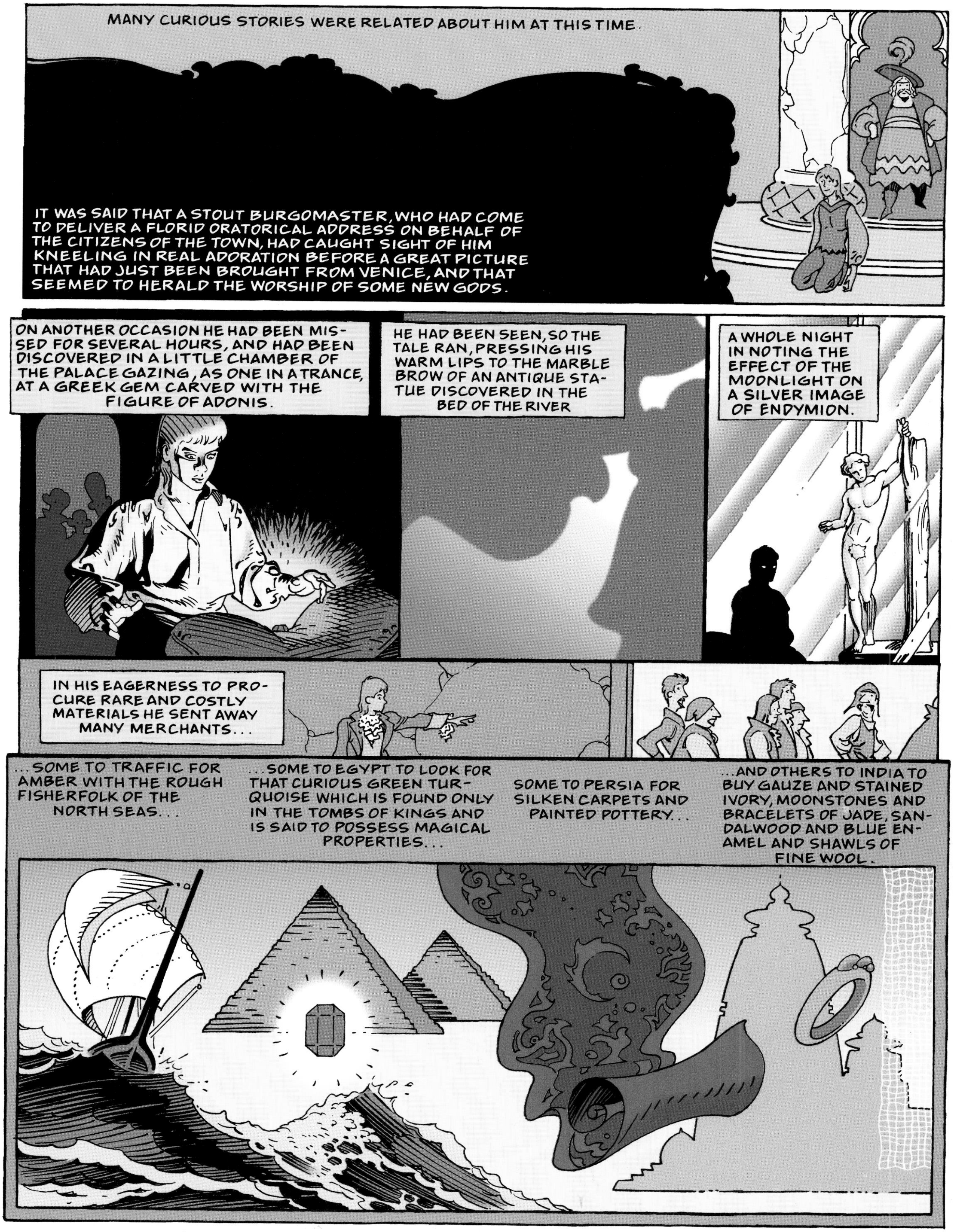
MANY CURIOUS STORIES WERE RELATED ABOUT HIM AT THIS TIME.
IT WAS SAID THAT A STOUT BURGOMASTER, WHO HAD COME TO DELIVER A FLORID ORATORICAL ADDRESS ON BEHALF OF THE CITIZENS OF THE TOWN, HAD CAUGHT SIGHT OF HIM KNEELING IN REAL ADORATION BEFORE A GREAT PICTURE THAT HAD JUST BEEN BROUGHT FROM VENICE, AND THAT SEEMED TO HERALD THE WORSHIP OF SOME NEW GODS.
ON ANOTHER OCCASION HE HAD BEEN MISSED FOR SEVERAL HOURS, AND HAD BEEN DISCOVERED IN A LITTLE CHAMBER OF THE PALACE GAZING, AS ONE IN A TRANCE, AT A GREEK GEM CARVED WITH THE FIGURE OF ADONIS.
HE HAD BEEN SEEN, SO THE TALE RAN, PRESSING HIS WARM LIPS TO THE MARBLE BROW OF AN ANTIQUE STATUE DISCOVERED IN THE BED OF THE RIVER
A WHOLE NIGHT IN NOTING THE EFFECT OF THE MOONLIGHT ON A SILVER IMAGE OF ENDYMION.
IN HIS EAGERNESS TO PROCURE RARE AND COSTLY MATERIALS HE SENT AWAY MANY MERCHANTS...
...SOME TO TRAFFIC FOR AMBER WITH THE ROUGH FISHERFOLK OF THE NORTH SEAS...
...SOME TO EGYPT TO LOOK FOR THAT CURIOUS GREEN TURQUOISE WHICH IS FOUND ONLY IN THE TOMBS OF KINGS AND IS SAID TO POSSESS MAGICAL PROPERTIES...
SOME TO PERSIA FOR SILKEN CARPETS AND PAINTED POTTERY...
...AND OTHERS TO INDIA TO BUY GAUZE AND STAINED IVORY, MOONSTONES AND BRACELETS OF JADE, SANDALWOOD AND BLUE ENAMEL AND SHAWLS OF FINE WOOL.

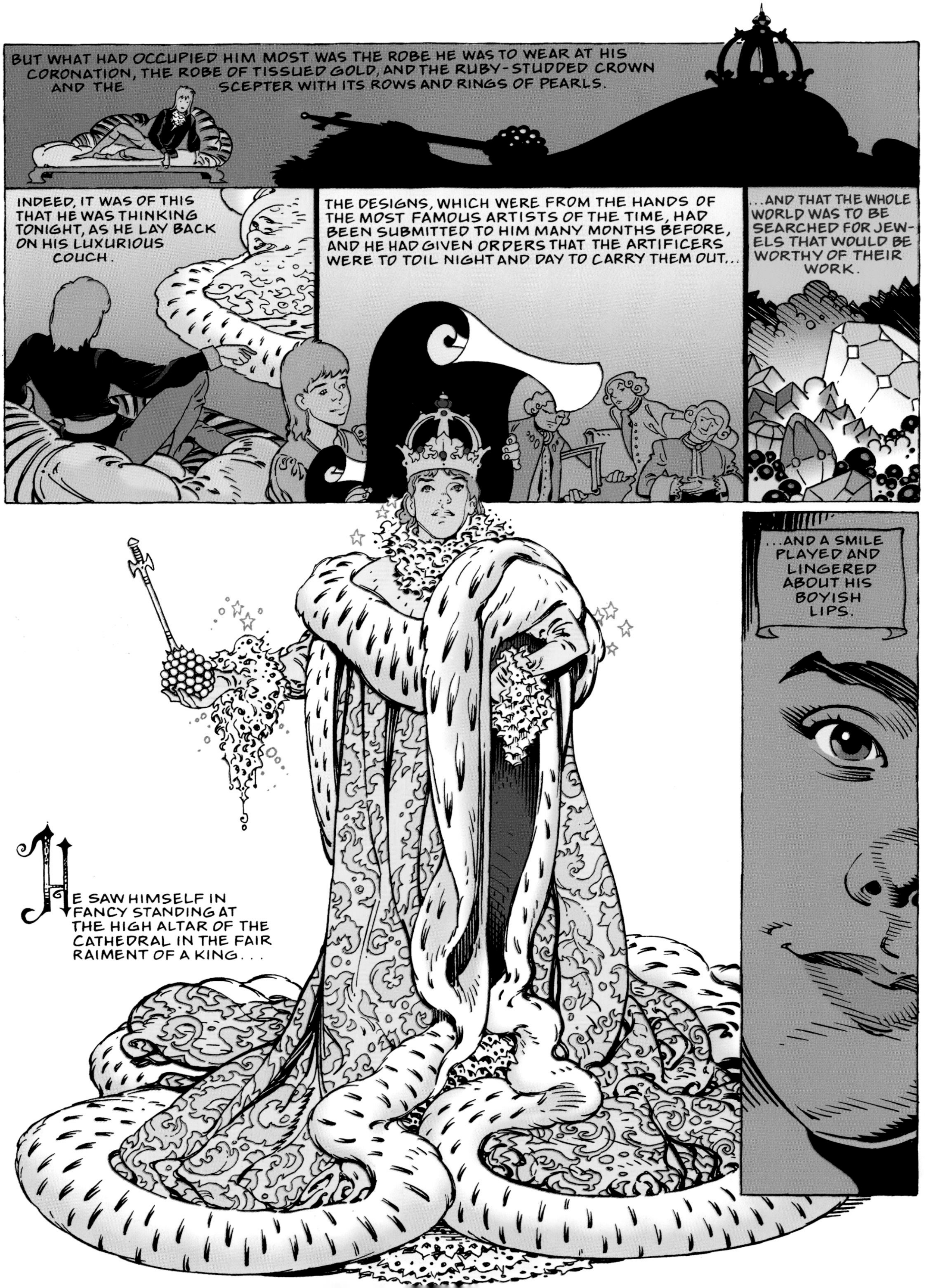
BUT WHAT HAD OCCUPIED HIM MOST WAS THE ROBE HE WAS TO WEAR AT HIS CORONATION, THE ROBE OF TISSUED GOLD, AND THE RUBY-STUDDED CROWN AND THE SCEPTER WITH ITS ROWS AND RINGS OF PEARLS.
INDEED, IT WAS OF THIS THAT HE WAS THINKING TONIGHT, AS HE LAY BACK ON HIS LUXURIOUS COUCH.
THE DESIGNS, WHICH WERE FROM THE HANDS OF THE MOST FAMOUS ARTISTS OF THE TIME, HAD BEEN SUBMITTED TO HIM MANY MONTHS BEFORE, AND HE HAD GIVEN ORDERS THAT THE ARTIFICERS WERE TO TOIL NIGHT AND DAY TO CARRY THEM OUT...
...AND THAT THE WHOLE WORLD WAS TO BE SEARCHED FOR JEWELS THAT WOULD BE WORTHY OF THEIR WORK.
HE SAW HIMSELF IN FANCY STANDING AT THE HIGH ALTAR OF THE CATHEDRAL IN THE FAIR RAIMENT OF A KING...
...AND A SMILE PLAYED AND LINGERED ABOUT HIS BOYISH LIPS.

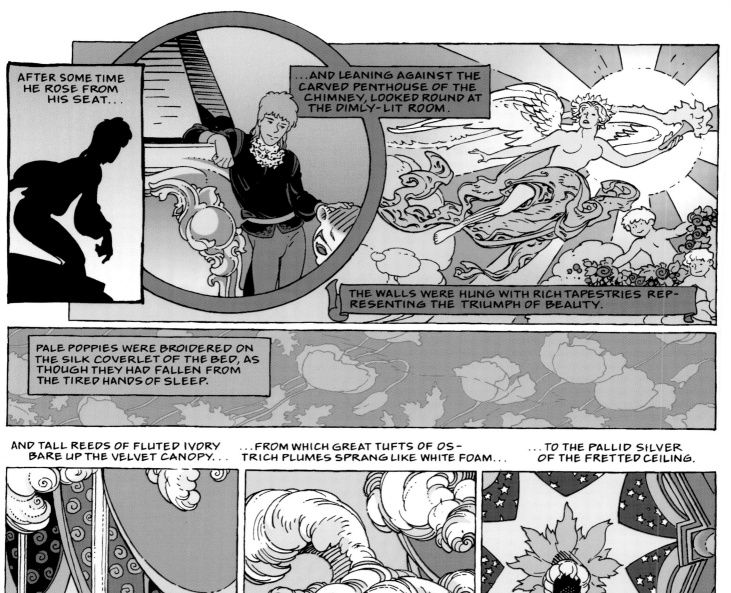

AFTER SOME TIME HE ROSE FROM HIS SEAT...

...AND LEANING AGAINST THE CARVED PENTHOUSE OF THE CHIMNEY, LOOKED ROUND AT THE DIMLY-LIT ROOM.

THE WALLS WERE HUNG WITH RICH TAPESTRIES REPRESENTING THE TRIUMPH OF BEAUTY.

PALE POPPIES WERE BROIDERED ON THE SILK COVERLET OF THE BED, AS THOUGH THEY HAD FALLEN FROM THE TIRED HANDS OF SLEEP.

AND TALL REEDS OF FLUTED IVORY BARE UP THE VELVET CANOPY...

...FROM WHICH GREAT TUFTS OF OSTRICH PLUMES SPRANG LIKE WHITE FOAM...

...TO THE PALLID SILVER OF THE FRETTED CEILING.

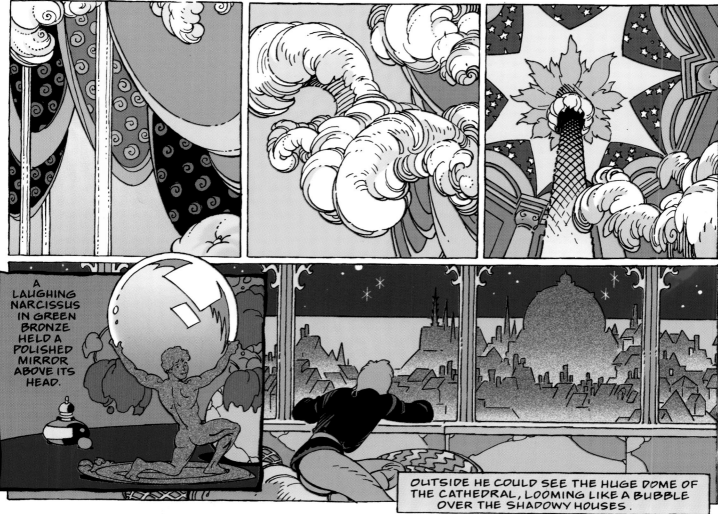

A LAUGHING NARCISSUS IN GREEN BRONZE HELD A POLISHED MIRROR ABOVE ITS HEAD.

OUTSIDE HE COULD SEE THE HUGE DOME OF THE CATHEDRAL, LOOMING LIKE A BUBBLE OVER THE SHADOWY HOUSES.

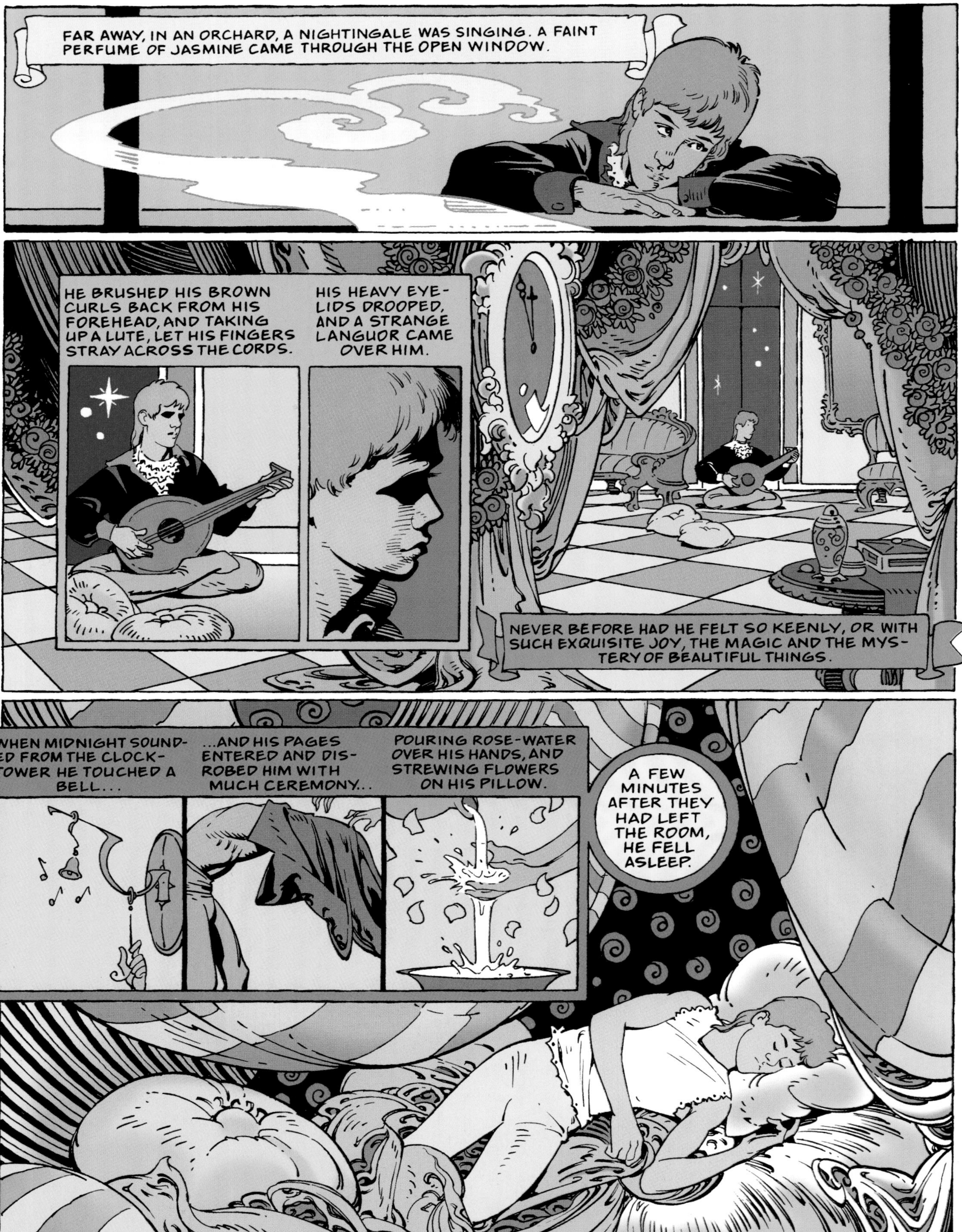
FAR AWAY, IN AN ORCHARD, A NIGHTINGALE WAS SINGING. A FAINT PERFUME OF JASMINE CAME THROUGH THE OPEN WINDOW.
HE BRUSHED HIS BROWN CURLS BACK FROM HIS FOREHEAD, AND TAKING UP A LUTE, LET HIS FINGERS STRAY ACROSS THE CORDS.
HIS HEAVY EYE-LIDS DROOPED, AND A STRANGE LANGUOR CAME OVER HIM.
NEVER BEFORE HAD HE FELT SO KEENLY, OR WITH SUCH EXQUISITE JOY, THE MAGIC AND THE MYSTERY OF BEAUTIFUL THINGS.
WHEN MIDNIGHT SOUNDED FROM THE CLOCK-TOWER HE TOUCHED A BELL...
...AND HIS PAGES ENTERED AND DISROBED HIM WITH MUCH CEREMONY...
POURING ROSE-WATER OVER HIS HANDS, AND STREWING FLOWERS ON HIS PILLOW.
A FEW MINUTES AFTER THEY HAD LEFT THE ROOM, HE FELL ASLEEP.

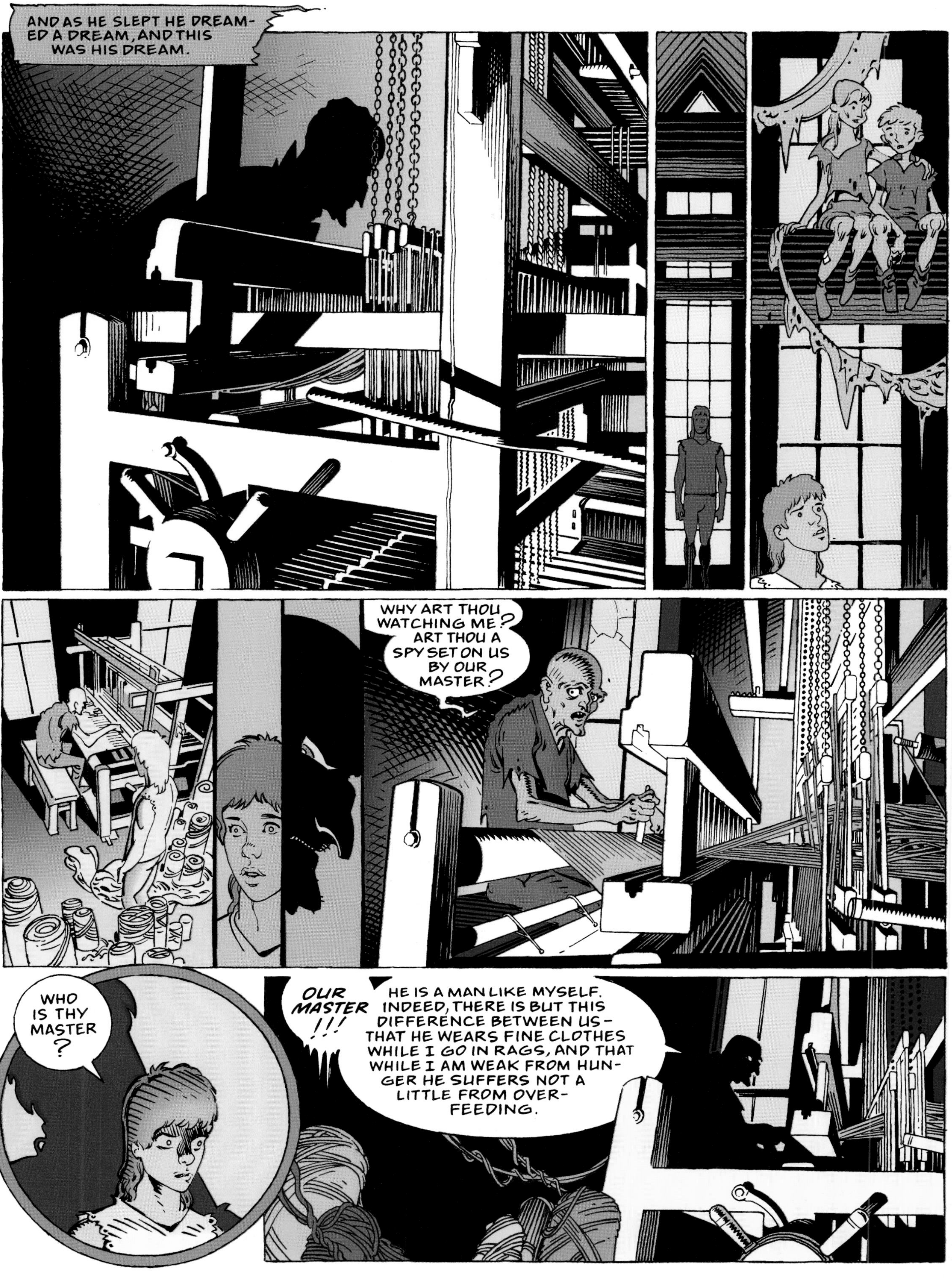
AND AS HE SLEPT HE DREAMED A DREAM, AND THIS WAS HIS DREAM.
WHY ART THOU WATCHING ME? ART THOU A SPY SET ON US BY OUR MASTER?
WHO IS THY MASTER?
OUR MASTER!!!
HE IS A MAN LIKE MYSELF. INDEED, THERE IS BUT THIS DIFFERENCE BETWEEN US – THAT HE WEARS FINE CLOTHES WHILE I GO IN RAGS, AND THAT WHILE I AM WEAK FROM HUNGER HE SUFFERS NOT A LITTLE FROM OVER-FEEDING.

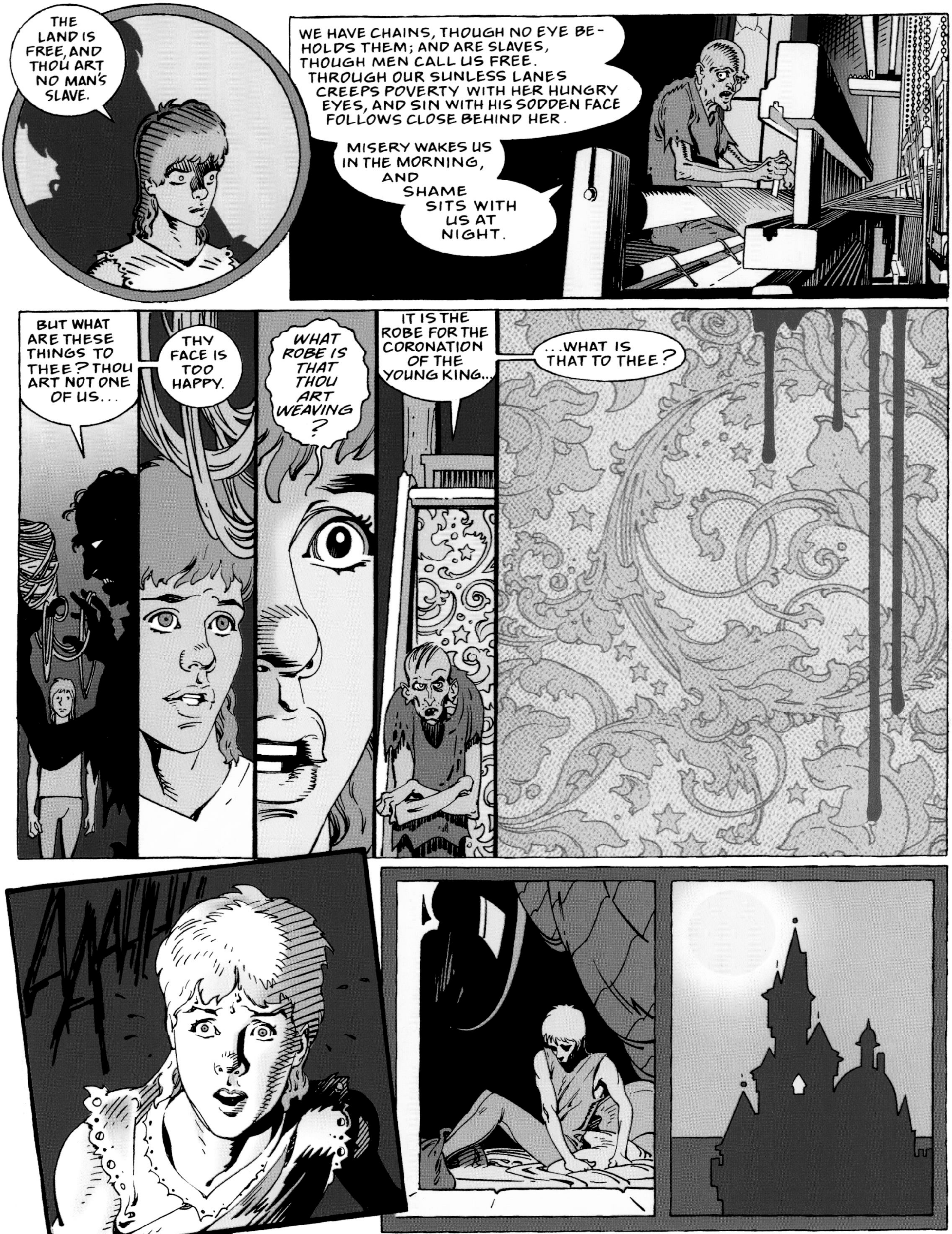
THE LAND IS FREE, AND THOU ART NO MAN'S SLAVE.
WE HAVE CHAINS, THOUGH NO EYE BEHOLDS THEM; AND ARE SLAVES, THOUGH MEN CALL US FREE. THROUGH OUR SUNLESS LANES CREEPS POVERTY WITH HER HUNGRY EYES, AND SIN WITH HIS SODDEN FACE FOLLOWS CLOSE BEHIND HER.
MISERY WAKES US IN THE MORNING, AND SHAME SITS WITH US AT NIGHT.
BUT WHAT ARE THESE THINGS TO THEE? THOU ART NOT ONE OF US...
THY FACE IS TOO HAPPY.
WHAT ROBE IS THAT THOU ART WEAVING?
IT IS THE ROBE FOR THE CORONATION OF THE YOUNG KING...
...WHAT IS THAT TO THEE?

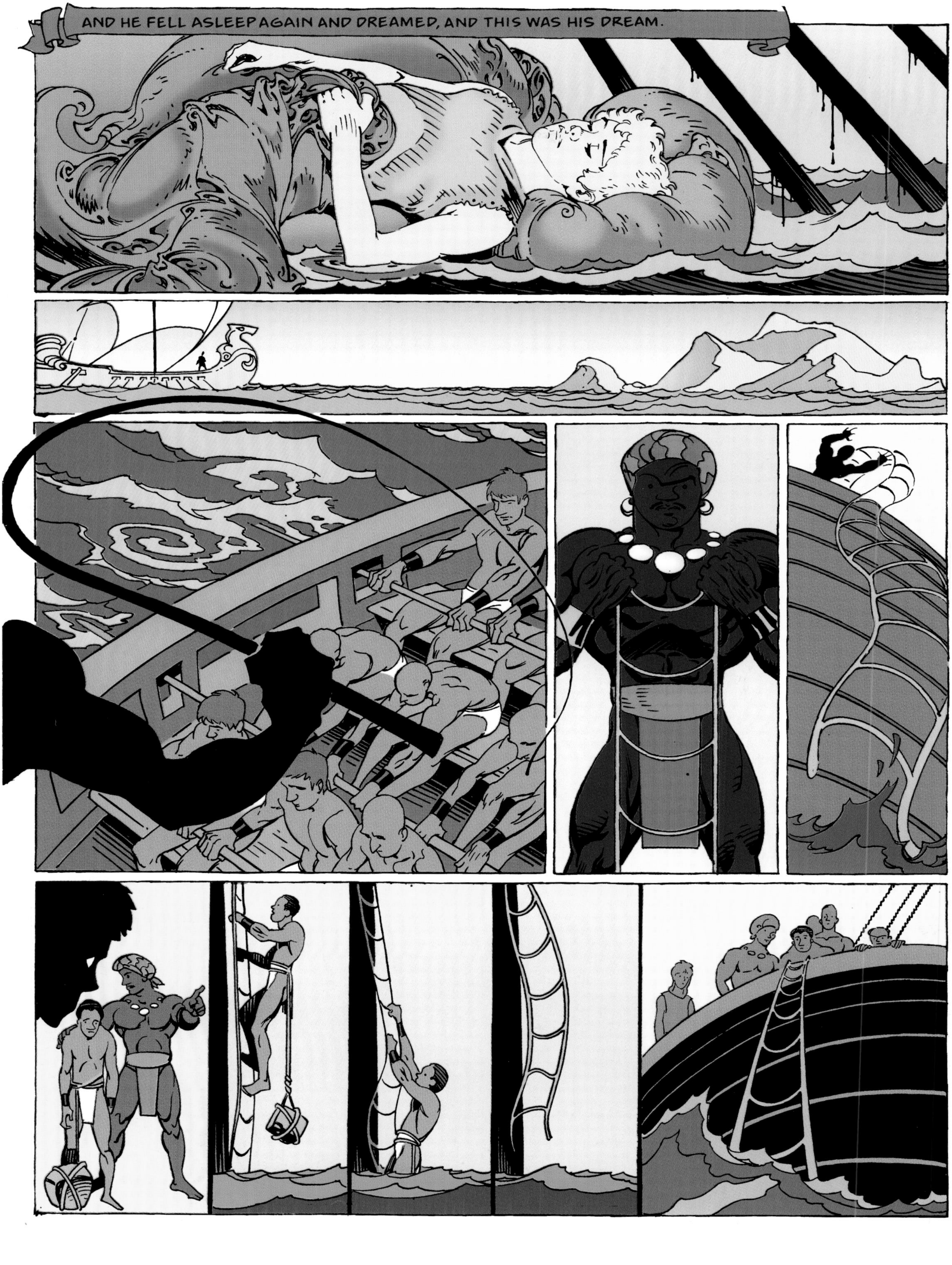
AND HE FELL ASLEEP AGAIN AND DREAMED, AND THIS WAS HIS DREAM.

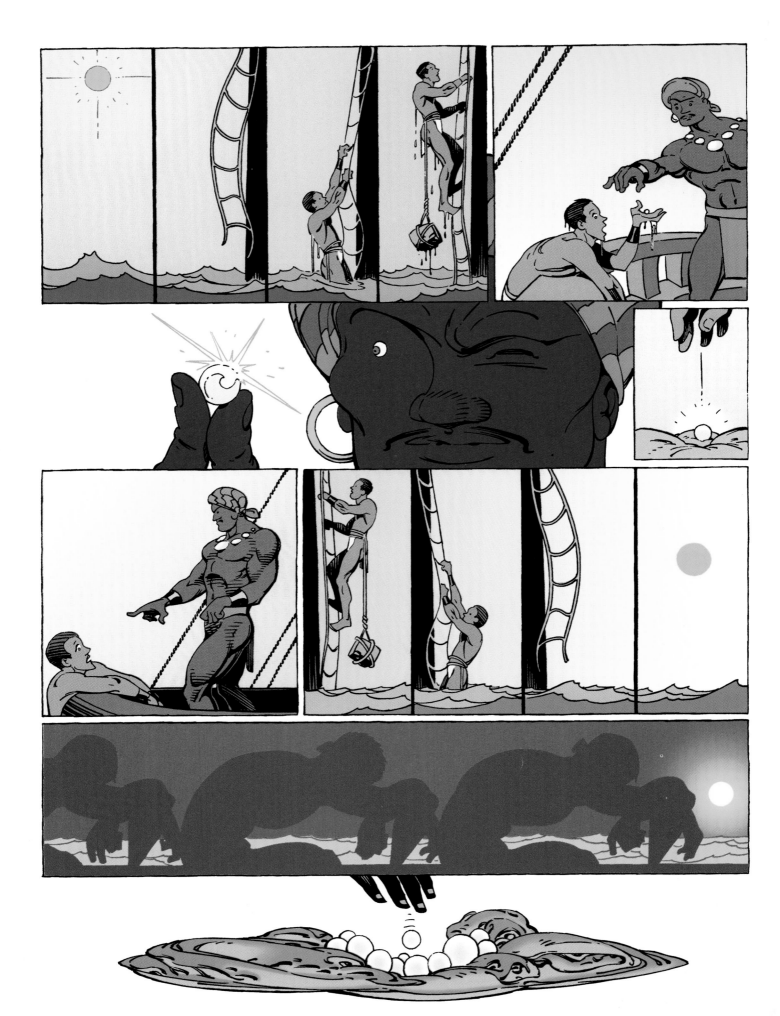

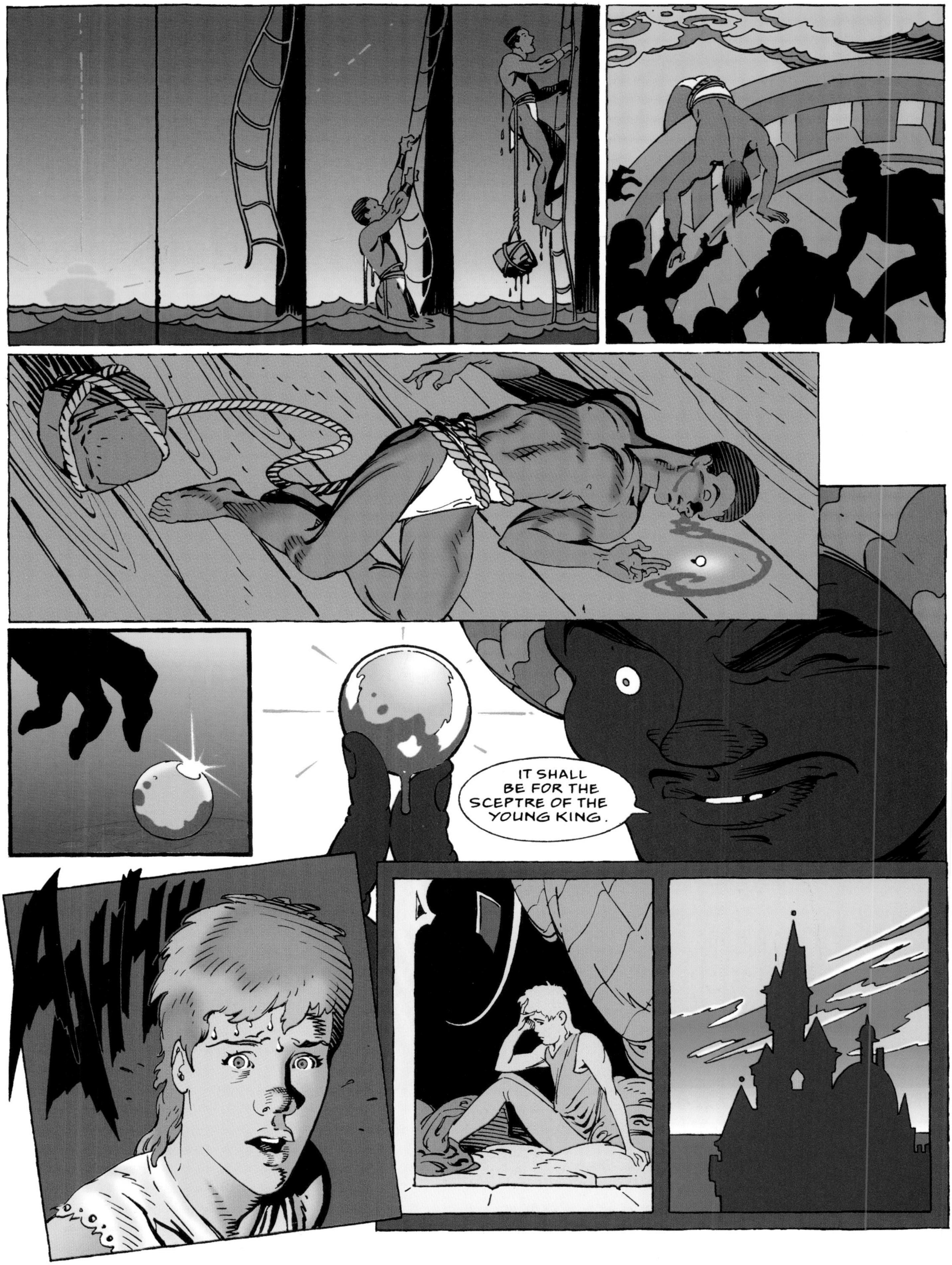
IT SHALL BE FOR THE SCEPTRE OF THE YOUNG KING.
AAHHH

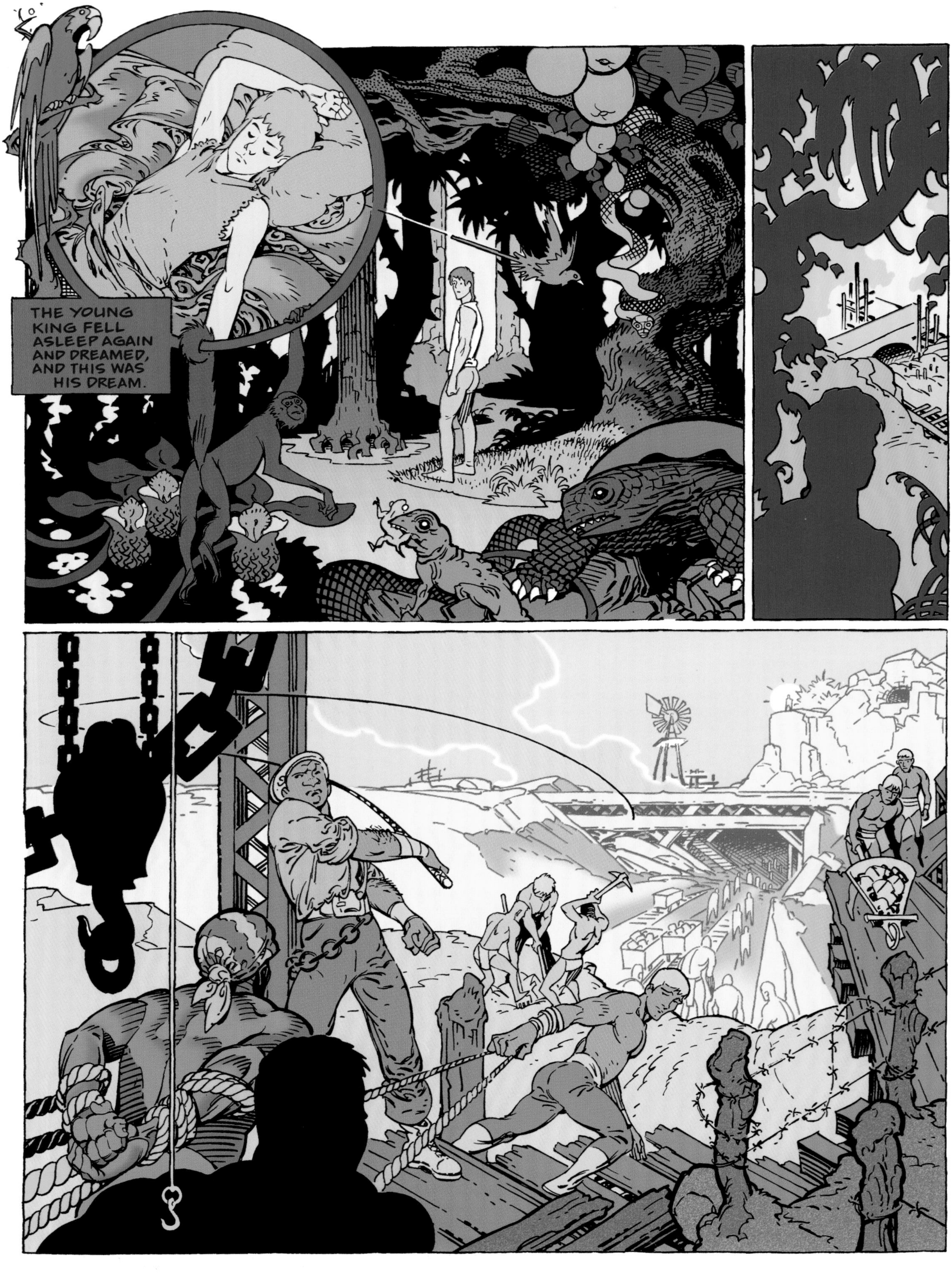
THE YOUNG KING FELL ASLEEP AGAIN AND DREAMED, AND THIS WAS HIS DREAM.

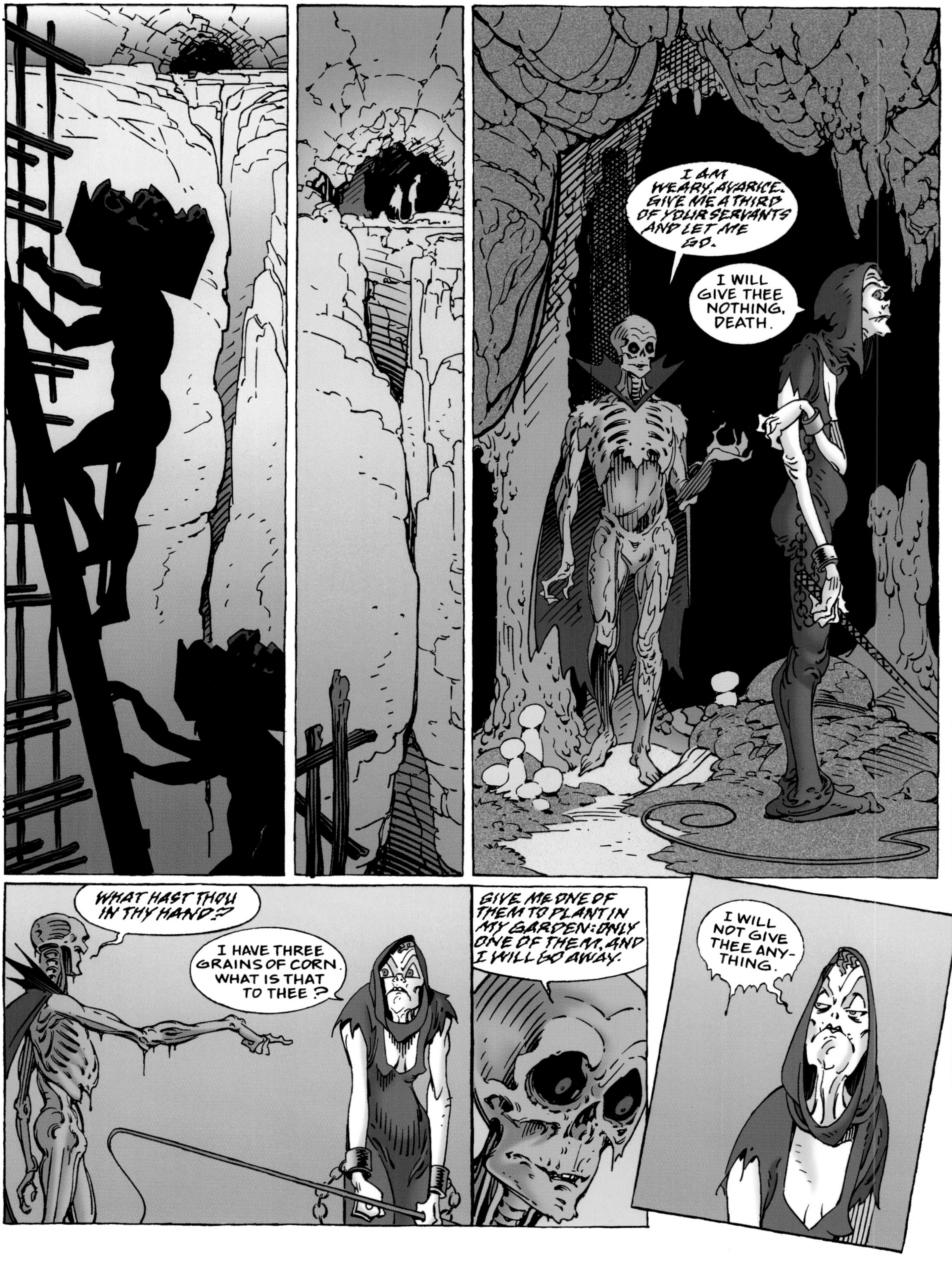
I AM WEARY, AVARICE. GIVE ME A THIRD OF YOUR SERVANTS AND LET ME GO.
I WILL GIVE THEE NOTHING, DEATH.
WHAT HAST THOU IN THY HAND?
I HAVE THREE GRAINS OF CORN. WHAT IS THAT TO THEE?
GIVE ME ONE OF THEM TO PLANT IN MY GARDEN: ONLY ONE OF THEM, AND I WILL GO AWAY.
I WILL NOT GIVE THEE ANY-THING.

VERY WELL.

AGUE!

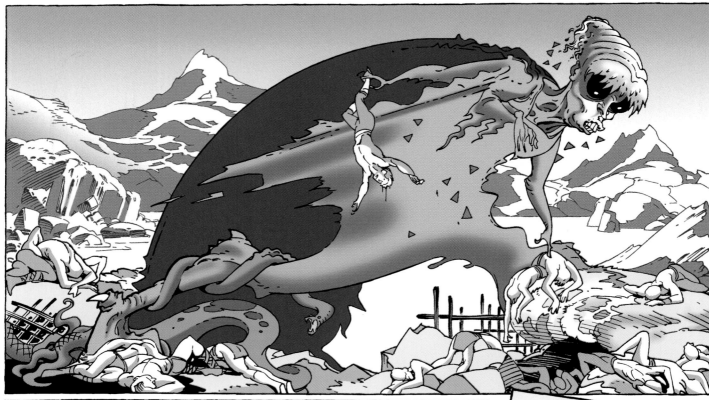

THOU HAST SLAIN A THIRD OF MY SERVANTS, GET THEE GONE. THERE IS WAR IN THE MOUNTAINS OF TARTARY, AND THE KINGS OF EACH SIDE ARE CALLING TO THEE.

WHAT IS MY VALLEY TO THEE, THAT THOU SHOULDST TARRY IN IT? GET THEE GONE, AND COME HERE NO MORE.

NAY, BUT TILL THOU HAST GIVEN ME A GRAIN OF CORN I WILL NOT GO.

I WILL NOT GIVE THEE ANYTHING.

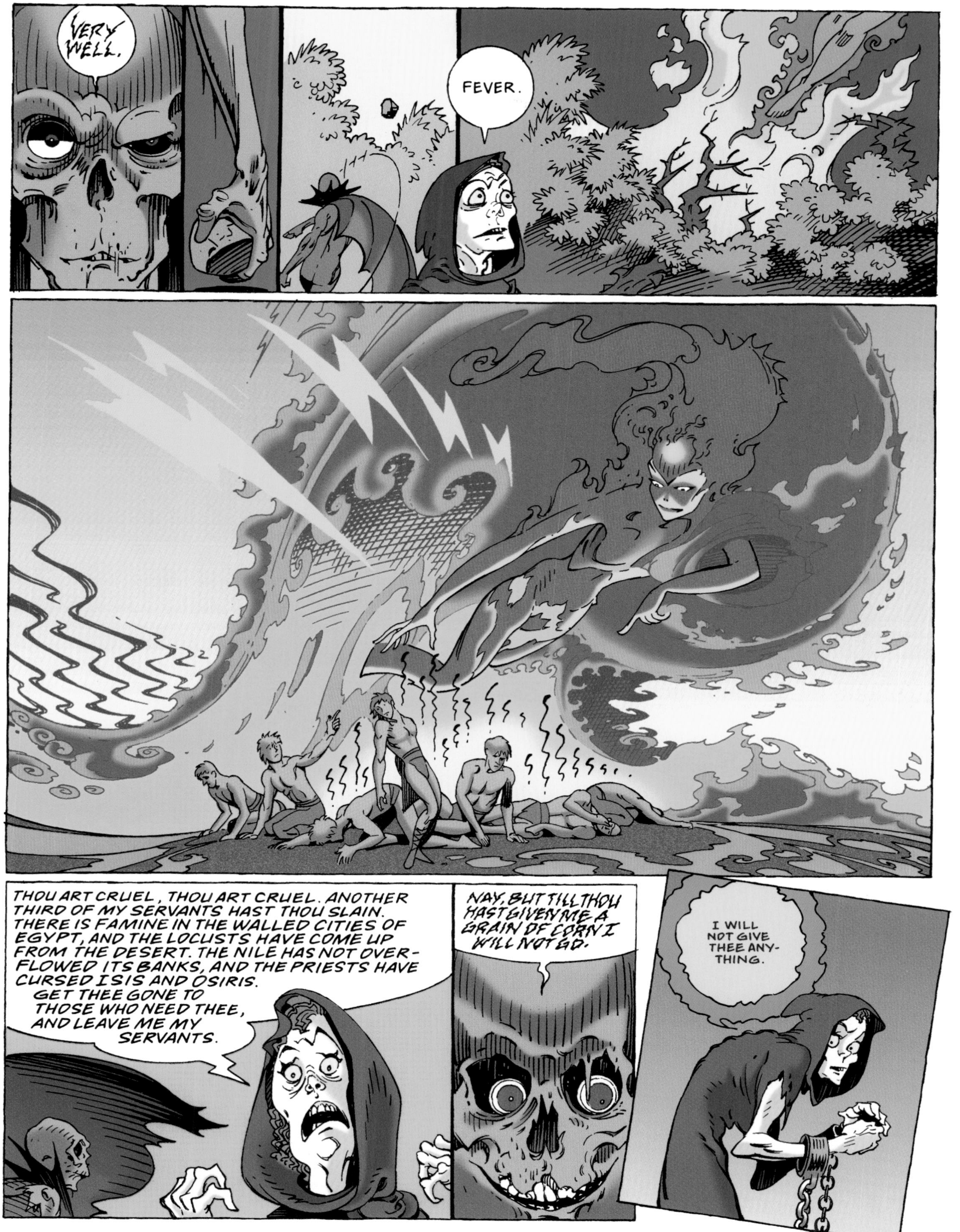
VERY WELL.
FEVER.
THOU ART CRUEL, THOU ART CRUEL. ANOTHER THIRD OF MY SERVANTS HAST THOU SLAIN. THERE IS FAMINE IN THE WALLED CITIES OF EGYPT, AND THE LOCUSTS HAVE COME UP FROM THE DESERT. THE NILE HAS NOT OVERFLOWED ITS BANKS, AND THE PRIESTS HAVE CURSED ISIS AND OSIRIS.
GET THEE GONE TO THOSE WHO NEED THEE, AND LEAVE ME MY SERVANTS.
NAY, BUT TILL THOU HAST GIVEN ME A GRAIN OF CORN I WILL NOT GO.
I WILL NOT GIVE THEE ANYTHING.

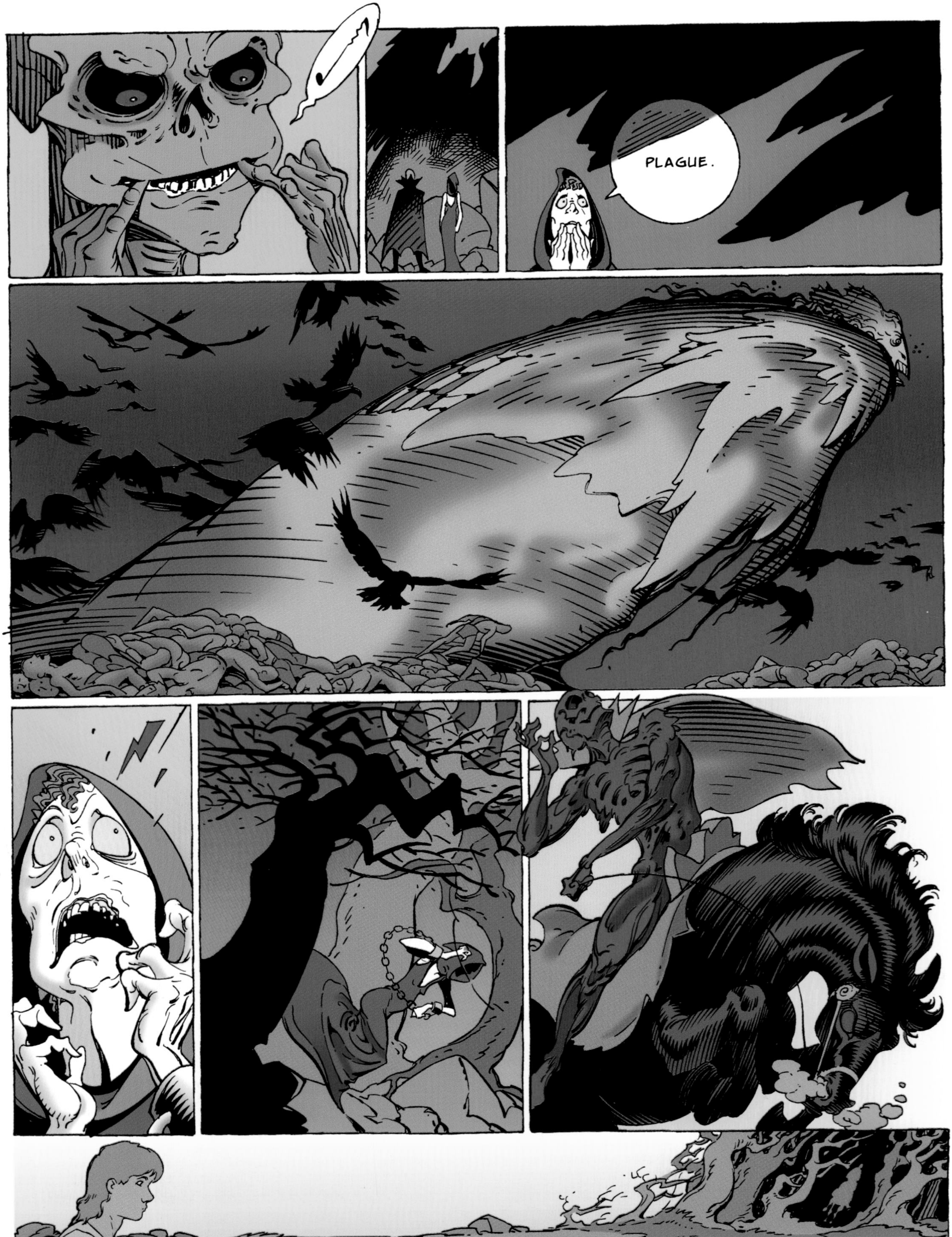
PLAGUE.

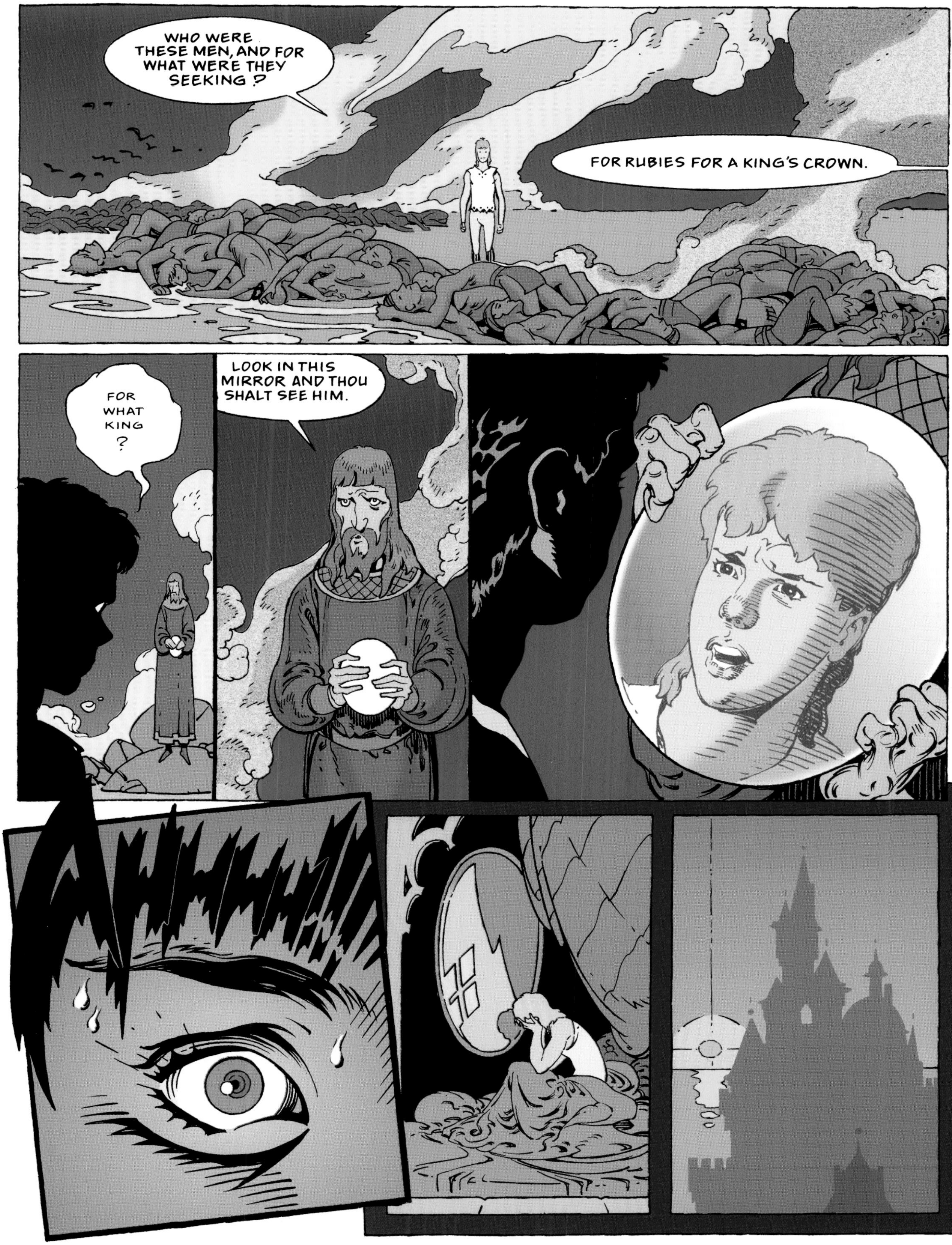

WHO WERE THESE MEN, AND FOR WHAT WERE THEY SEEKING?
FOR RUBIES FOR A KING'S CROWN.
FOR WHAT KING?
LOOK IN THIS MIRROR AND THOU SHALT SEE HIM.

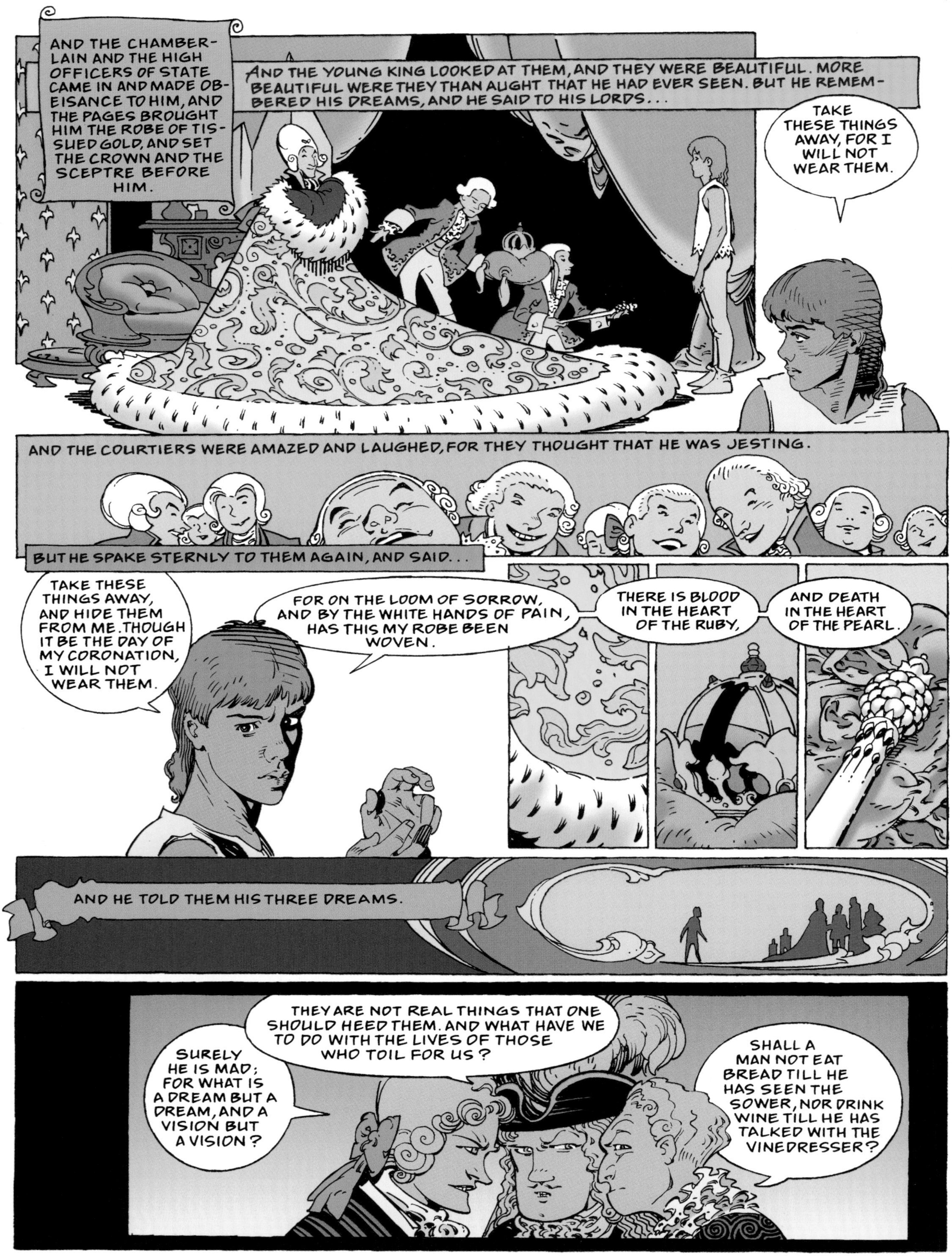
AND THE CHAMBERLAIN AND THE HIGH OFFICERS OF STATE CAME IN AND MADE OBEISANCE TO HIM, AND THE PAGES BROUGHT HIM THE ROBE OF TISSUED GOLD, AND SET THE CROWN AND THE SCEPTRE BEFORE HIM.
AND THE YOUNG KING LOOKED AT THEM, AND THEY WERE BEAUTIFUL. MORE BEAUTIFUL WERE THEY THAN AUGHT THAT HE HAD EVER SEEN. BUT HE REMEMBERED HIS DREAMS, AND HE SAID TO HIS LORDS...
TAKE THESE THINGS AWAY, FOR I WILL NOT WEAR THEM.
AND THE COURTIERS WERE AMAZED AND LAUGHED, FOR THEY THOUGHT THAT HE WAS JESTING.
BUT HE SPAKE STERNLY TO THEM AGAIN, AND SAID...
TAKE THESE THINGS AWAY, AND HIDE THEM FROM ME. THOUGH IT BE THE DAY OF MY CORONATION, I WILL NOT WEAR THEM.
FOR ON THE LOOM OF SORROW, AND BY THE WHITE HANDS OF PAIN, HAS THIS MY ROBE BEEN WOVEN.
THERE IS BLOOD IN THE HEART OF THE RUBY,
AND DEATH IN THE HEART OF THE PEARL.
AND HE TOLD THEM HIS THREE DREAMS.
SURELY HE IS MAD; FOR WHAT IS A DREAM BUT A DREAM, AND A VISION BUT A VISION?
THEY ARE NOT REAL THINGS THAT ONE SHOULD HEED THEM. AND WHAT HAVE WE TO DO WITH THE LIVES OF THOSE WHO TOIL FOR US?
SHALL A MAN NOT EAT BREAD TILL HE HAS SEEN THE SOWER, NOR DRINK WINE TILL HE HAS TALKED WITH THE VINEDRESSER?

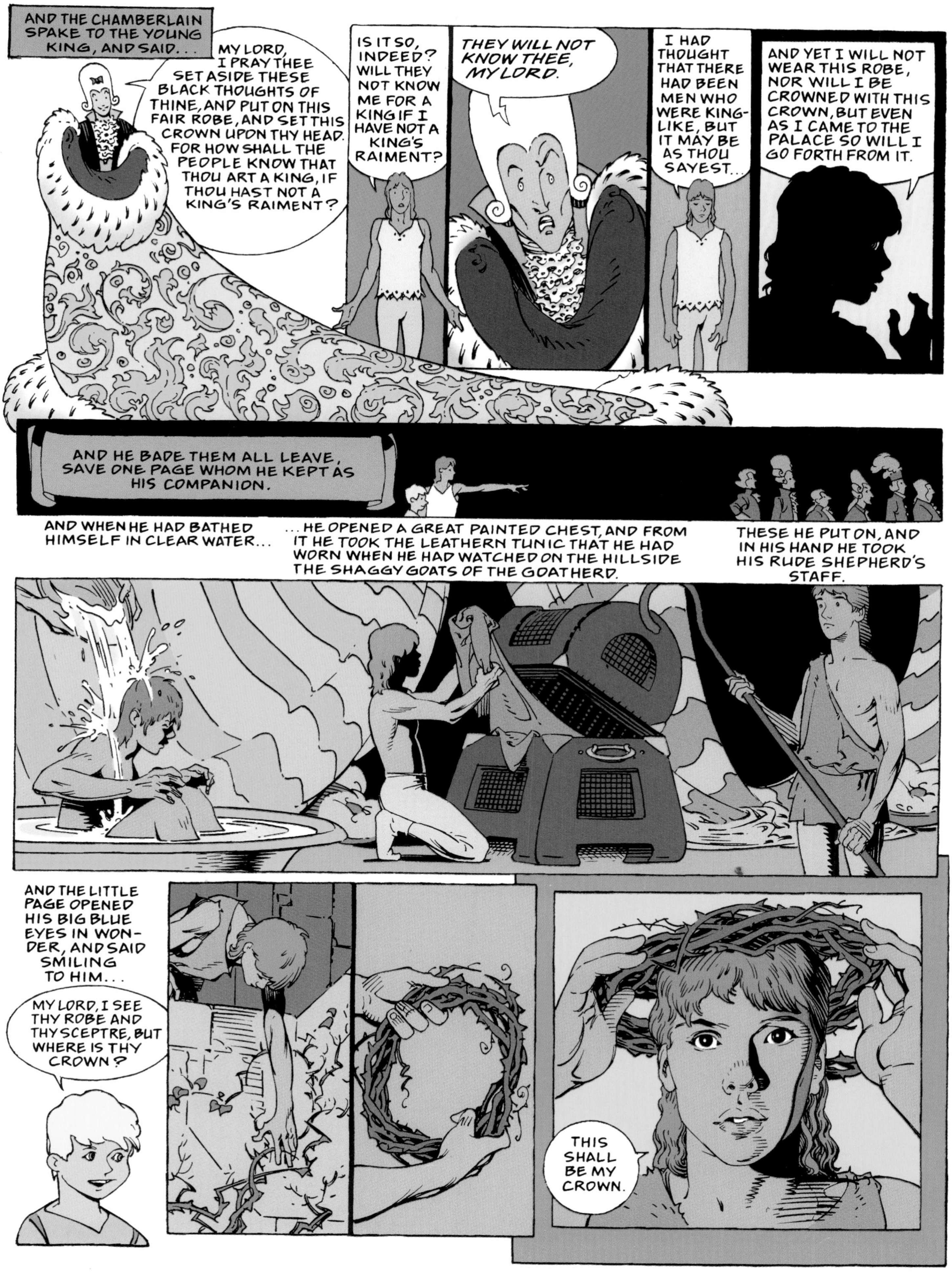
AND THE CHAMBERLAIN SPAKE TO THE YOUNG KING, AND SAID...
MY LORD, I PRAY THEE SET ASIDE THESE BLACK THOUGHTS OF THINE, AND PUT ON THIS FAIR ROBE, AND SET THIS CROWN UPON THY HEAD. FOR HOW SHALL THE PEOPLE KNOW THAT THOU ART A KING, IF THOU HAST NOT A KING'S RAIMENT?
IS IT SO, INDEED? WILL THEY NOT KNOW ME FOR A KING IF I HAVE NOT A KING'S RAIMENT?
THEY WILL NOT KNOW THEE, MY LORD.
I HAD THOUGHT THAT THERE HAD BEEN MEN WHO WERE KING-LIKE, BUT IT MAY BE AS THOU SAYEST...
AND YET I WILL NOT WEAR THIS ROBE, NOR WILL I BE CROWNED WITH THIS CROWN, BUT EVEN AS I CAME TO THE PALACE SO WILL I GO FORTH FROM IT.
AND HE BADE THEM ALL LEAVE, SAVE ONE PAGE WHOM HE KEPT AS HIS COMPANION.
AND WHEN HE HAD BATHED HIMSELF IN CLEAR WATER...
...HE OPENED A GREAT PAINTED CHEST, AND FROM IT HE TOOK THE LEATHERN TUNIC THAT HE HAD WORN WHEN HE HAD WATCHED ON THE HILLSIDE THE SHAGGY GOATS OF THE GOATHERD.
THESE HE PUT ON, AND IN HIS HAND HE TOOK HIS RUDE SHEPHERD'S STAFF.
AND THE LITTLE PAGE OPENED HIS BIG BLUE EYES IN WONDER, AND SAID SMILING TO HIM...
MY LORD, I SEE THY ROBE AND THY SCEPTRE, BUT WHERE IS THY CROWN?
THIS SHALL BE MY CROWN.

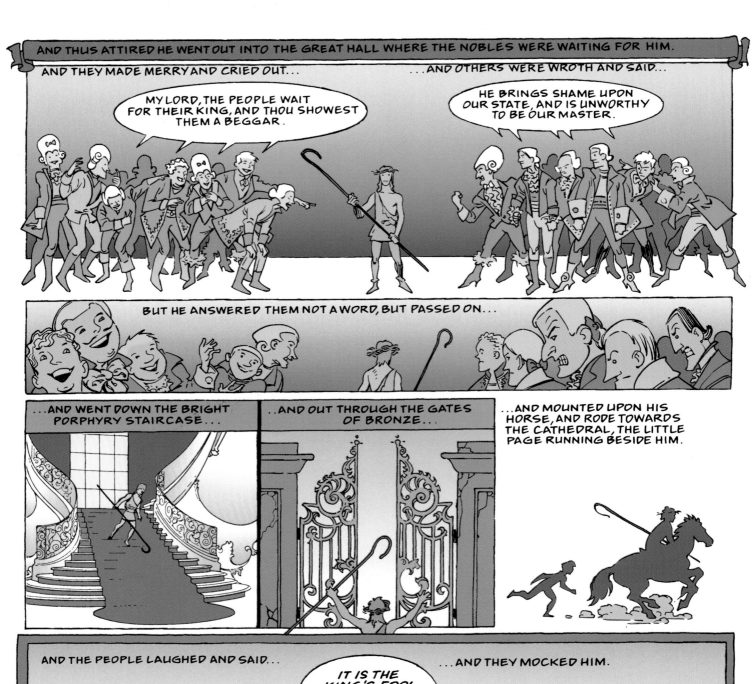

AND THUS ATTIRED HE WENT OUT INTO THE GREAT HALL WHERE THE NOBLES WERE WAITING FOR HIM.

AND THEY MADE MERRY AND CRIED OUT...

...AND OTHERS WERE WROTH AND SAID...

MY LORD, THE PEOPLE WAIT FOR THEIR KING, AND THOU SHOWEST THEM A BEGGAR.

HE BRINGS SHAME UPON OUR STATE, AND IS UNWORTHY TO BE OUR MASTER.

BUT HE ANSWERED THEM NOT A WORD, BUT PASSED ON...

...AND WENT DOWN THE BRIGHT PORPHYRY STAIRCASE...

...AND OUT THROUGH THE GATES OF BRONZE...

...AND MOUNTED UPON HIS HORSE, AND RODE TOWARDS THE CATHEDRAL, THE LITTLE PAGE RUNNING BESIDE HIM.

AND THE PEOPLE LAUGHED AND SAID...

...AND THEY MOCKED HIM.

IT IS THE KING'S FOOL WHO IS RIDING BY!

AND HE DREW REIN AND SAID...

NAY, BUT I AM THE KING.

...AND HE TOLD THEM HIS THREE DREAMS.

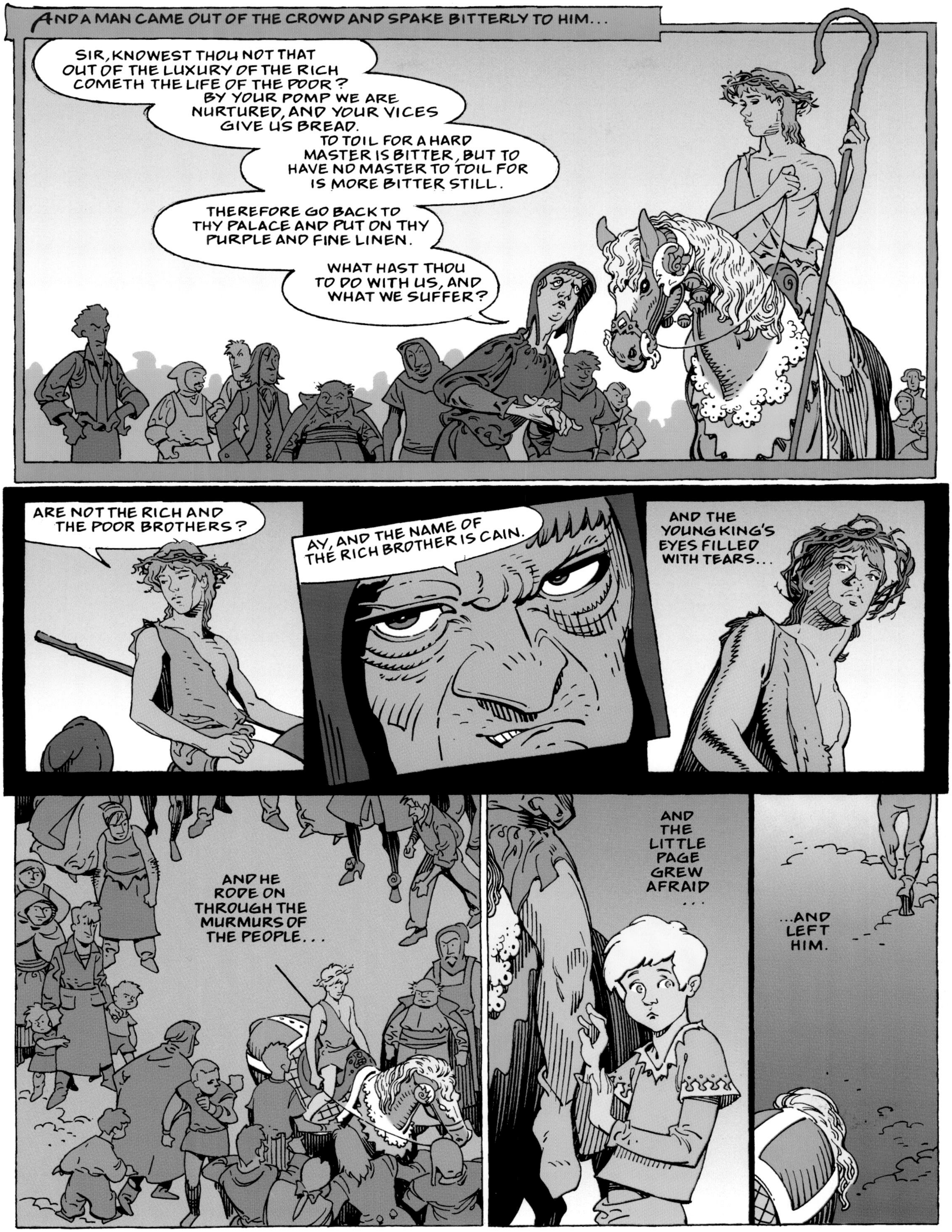
AND A MAN CAME OUT OF THE CROWD AND SPAKE BITTERLY TO HIM...
SIR, KNOWEST THOU NOT THAT OUT OF THE LUXURY OF THE RICH COMETH THE LIFE OF THE POOR?
BY YOUR POMP WE ARE NURTURED, AND YOUR VICES GIVE US BREAD.
TO TOIL FOR A HARD MASTER IS BITTER, BUT TO HAVE NO MASTER TO TOIL FOR IS MORE BITTER STILL.
THEREFORE GO BACK TO THY PALACE AND PUT ON THY PURPLE AND FINE LINEN.
WHAT HAST THOU TO DO WITH US, AND WHAT WE SUFFER?
ARE NOT THE RICH AND THE POOR BROTHERS?
AY, AND THE NAME OF THE RICH BROTHER IS CAIN.
AND THE YOUNG KING'S EYES FILLED WITH TEARS...
AND HE RODE ON THROUGH THE MURMURS OF THE PEOPLE...
AND THE LITTLE PAGE GREW AFRAID...
...AND LEFT HIM.

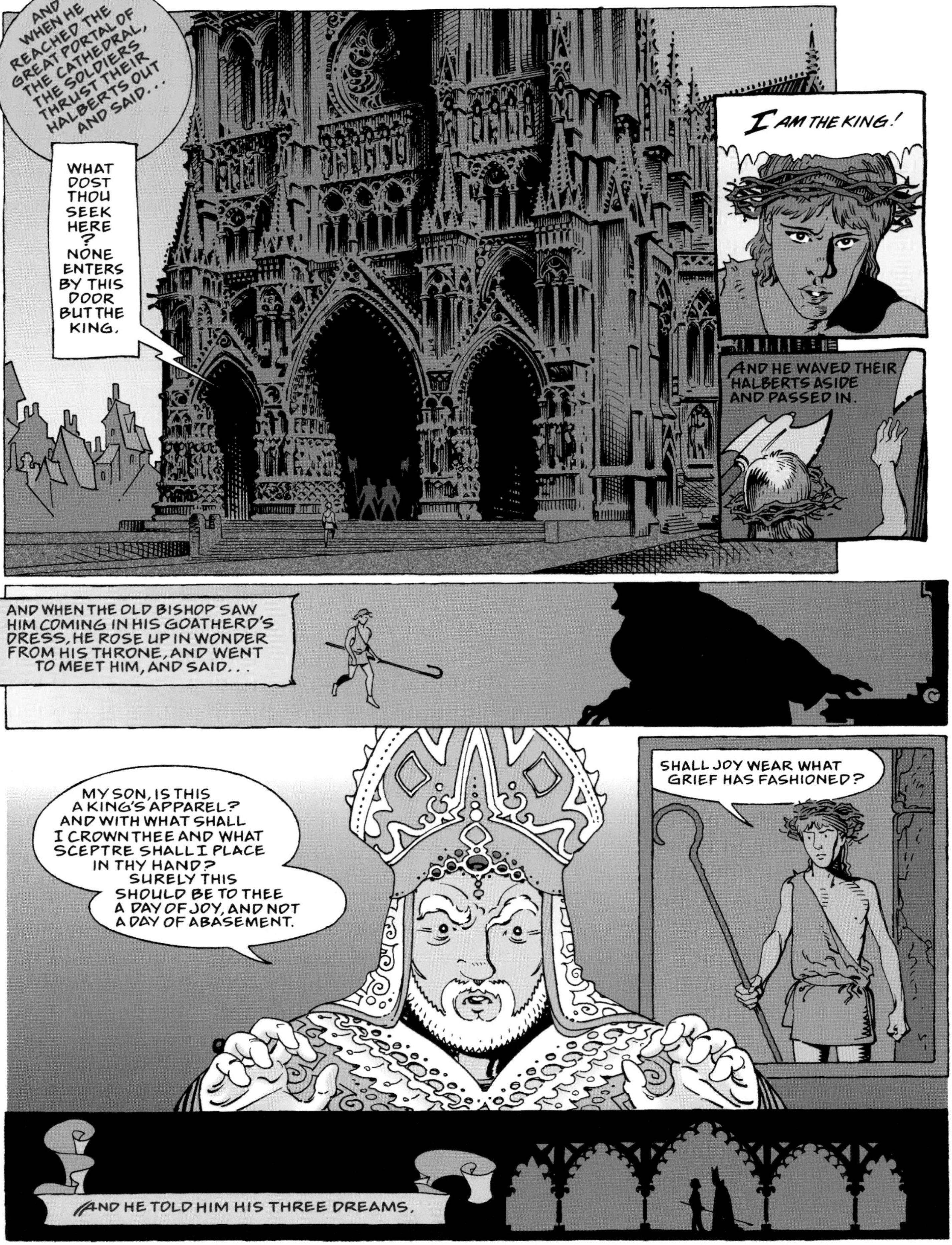
AND WHEN HE REACHED THE GREAT PORTAL OF THE CATHEDRAL, THE SOLDIERS THRUST THEIR HALBERTS OUT AND SAID...
WHAT DOST THOU SEEK HERE? NONE ENTERS BY THIS DOOR BUT THE KING.
I AM THE KING!
AND HE WAVED THEIR HALBERTS ASIDE AND PASSED IN.
AND WHEN THE OLD BISHOP SAW HIM COMING IN HIS GOATHERD'S DRESS, HE ROSE UP IN WONDER FROM HIS THRONE, AND WENT TO MEET HIM, AND SAID...
MY SON, IS THIS A KING'S APPAREL? AND WITH WHAT SHALL I CROWN THEE AND WHAT SCEPTRE SHALL I PLACE IN THY HAND? SURELY THIS SHOULD BE TO THEE A DAY OF JOY, AND NOT A DAY OF ABASEMENT.
SHALL JOY WEAR WHAT GRIEF HAS FASHIONED?
AND HE TOLD HIM HIS THREE DREAMS.

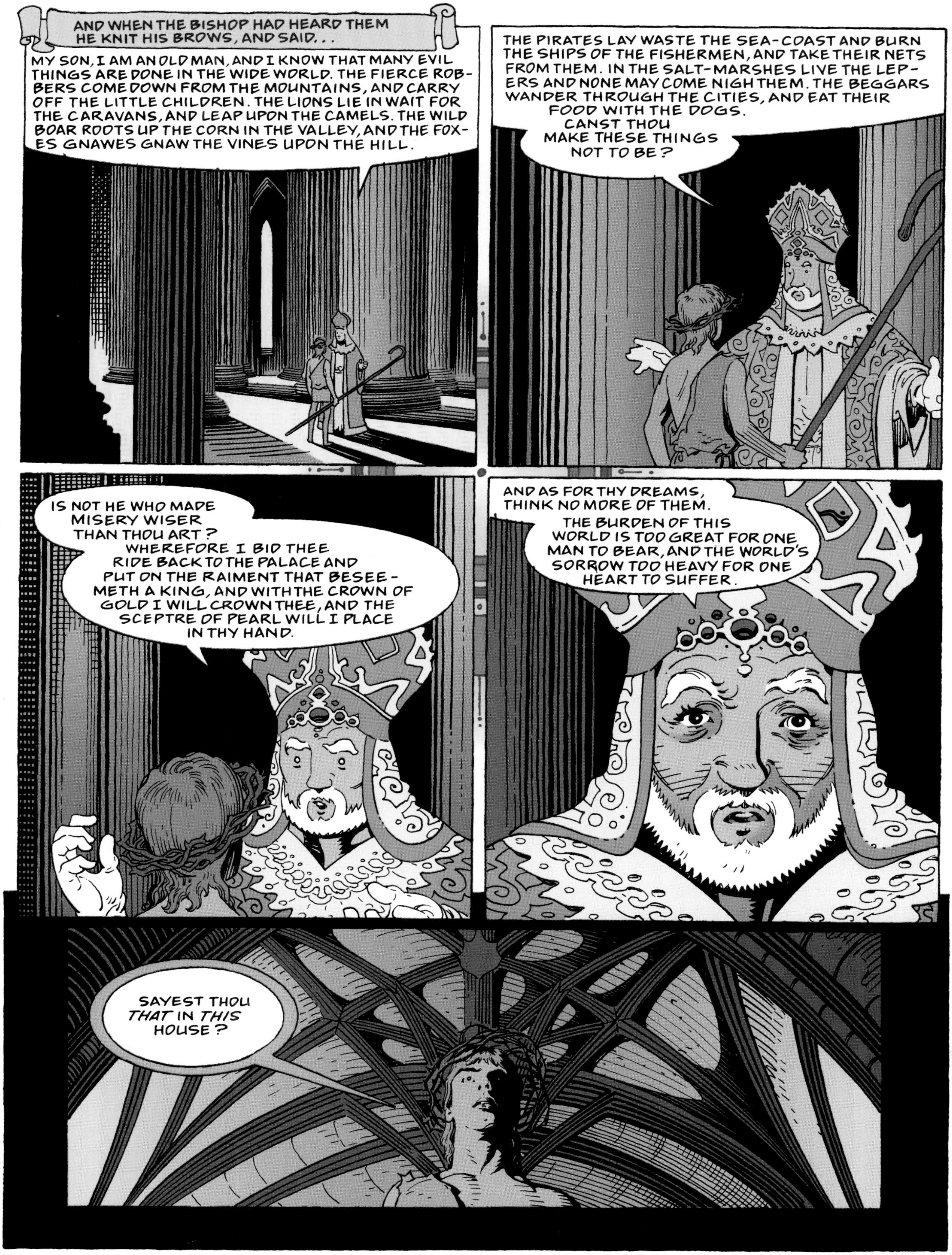
AND WHEN THE BISHOP HAD HEARD THEM HE KNIT HIS BROWS, AND SAID. . .
MY SON, I AM AN OLD MAN, AND I KNOW THAT MANY EVIL THINGS ARE DONE IN THE WIDE WORLD. THE FIERCE ROBBERS COME DOWN FROM THE MOUNTAINS, AND CARRY OFF THE LITTLE CHILDREN. THE LIONS LIE IN WAIT FOR THE CARAVANS, AND LEAP UPON THE CAMELS. THE WILD BOAR ROOTS UP THE CORN IN THE VALLEY, AND THE FOXES GNAWES GNAW THE VINES UPON THE HILL.
THE PIRATES LAY WASTE THE SEA-COAST AND BURN THE SHIPS OF THE FISHERMEN, AND TAKE THEIR NETS FROM THEM. IN THE SALT-MARSHES LIVE THE LEPERS AND NONE MAY COME NIGH THEM. THE BEGGARS WANDER THROUGH THE CITIES, AND EAT THEIR FOOD WITH THE DOGS.
CANST THOU MAKE THESE THINGS NOT TO BE?
IS NOT HE WHO MADE MISERY WISER THAN THOU ART? WHEREFORE I BID THEE RIDE BACK TO THE PALACE AND PUT ON THE RAIMENT THAT BESEEMETH A KING, AND WITH THE CROWN OF GOLD I WILL CROWN THEE, AND THE SCEPTRE OF PEARL WILL I PLACE IN THY HAND.
AND AS FOR THY DREAMS, THINK NO MORE OF THEM.
THE BURDEN OF THIS WORLD IS TOO GREAT FOR ONE MAN TO BEAR, AND THE WORLD'S SORROW TOO HEAVY FOR ONE HEART TO SUFFER.
SAYEST THOU *THAT* IN *THIS* HOUSE?

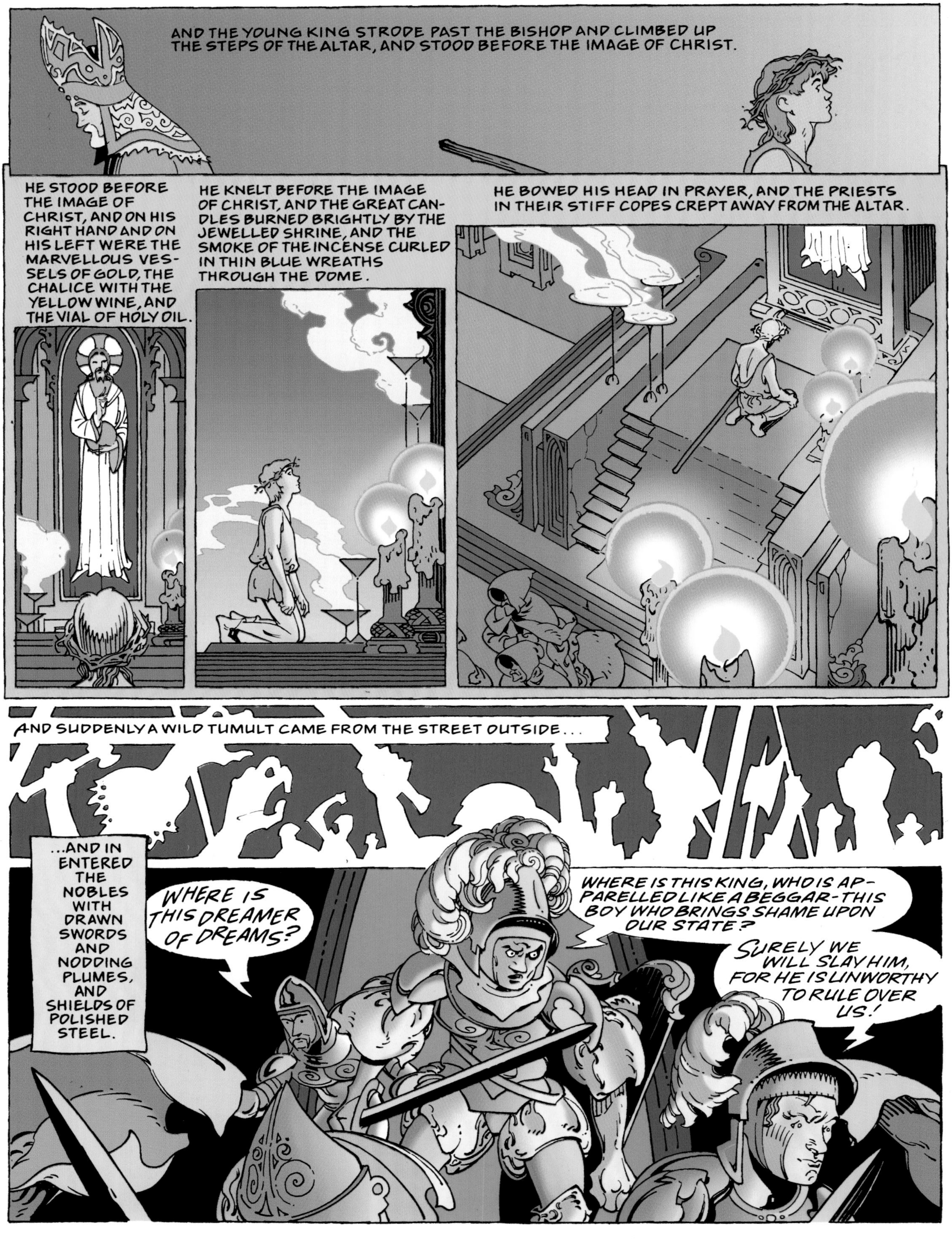
AND THE YOUNG KING STRODE PAST THE BISHOP AND CLIMBED UP THE STEPS OF THE ALTAR, AND STOOD BEFORE THE IMAGE OF CHRIST.
HE STOOD BEFORE THE IMAGE OF CHRIST, AND ON HIS RIGHT HAND AND ON HIS LEFT WERE THE MARVELLOUS VESSELS OF GOLD, THE CHALICE WITH THE YELLOW WINE, AND THE VIAL OF HOLY OIL.
HE KNELT BEFORE THE IMAGE OF CHRIST, AND THE GREAT CANDLES BURNED BRIGHTLY BY THE JEWELLED SHRINE, AND THE SMOKE OF THE INCENSE CURLED IN THIN BLUE WREATHS THROUGH THE DOME.
HE BOWED HIS HEAD IN PRAYER, AND THE PRIESTS IN THEIR STIFF COPES CREPT AWAY FROM THE ALTAR.
AND SUDDENLY A WILD TUMULT CAME FROM THE STREET OUTSIDE...
...AND IN ENTERED THE NOBLES WITH DRAWN SWORDS AND NODDING PLUMES, AND SHIELDS OF POLISHED STEEL.
WHERE IS THIS DREAMER OF DREAMS?
WHERE IS THIS KING, WHO IS APPARELLED LIKE A BEGGAR-THIS BOY WHO BRINGS SHAME UPON OUR STATE?
SURELY WE WILL SLAY HIM, FOR HE IS UNWORTHY TO RULE OVER US!

AND THE YOUNG KING BOWED HIS HEAD AGAIN, AND PRAYED...

...AND WHEN HE HAD FINISHED HIS PRAYER...

HE ROSE UP, AND — TURNING ROUND HE LOOKED AT THEM SADLY.

AND LO!...

THROUGH THE PAINTED WINDOWS CAME THE SUNLIGHT STREAMING UPON HIM, AND THE SUN-BEAMS WOVE ROUND HIM A TISSUED ROBE THAT WAS FAIRER THAN THE ROBE THAT HAD BEEN FASHIONED FOR HIS PLEASURE.

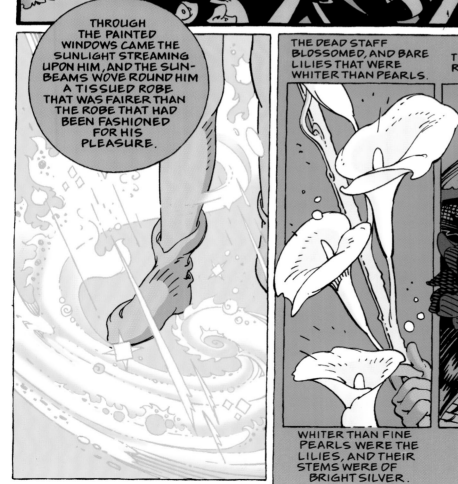

THE DEAD STAFF BLOSSOMED, AND BARE LILIES THAT WERE WHITER THAN PEARLS.

WHITER THAN FINE PEARLS WERE THE LILIES, AND THEIR STEMS WERE OF BRIGHT SILVER.

THE DRY THORN BLOSSOMED, AND BARE ROSES THAT WERE REDDER THAN RUBIES.

REDDER THAN MALE RUBIES WERE THE ROSES, AND THEIR LEAVES WERE OF BEATEN GOLD.

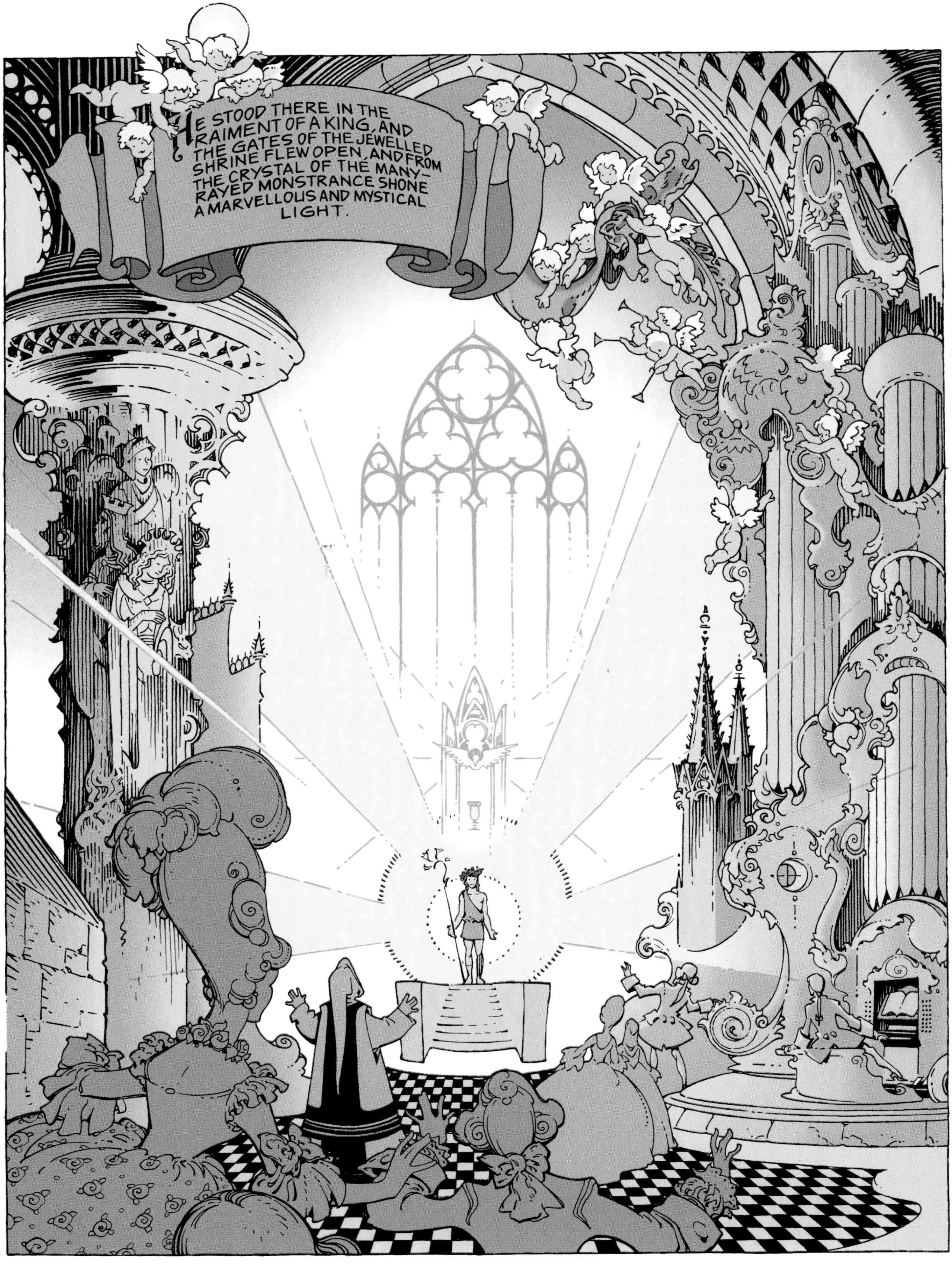
HE STOOD THERE IN THE RAIMENT OF A KING, AND THE GATES OF THE JEWELLED SHRINE FLEW OPEN, AND FROM THE CRYSTAL OF THE MANY-RAYED MONSTRANCE SHONE A MARVELLOUS AND MYSTICAL LIGHT.

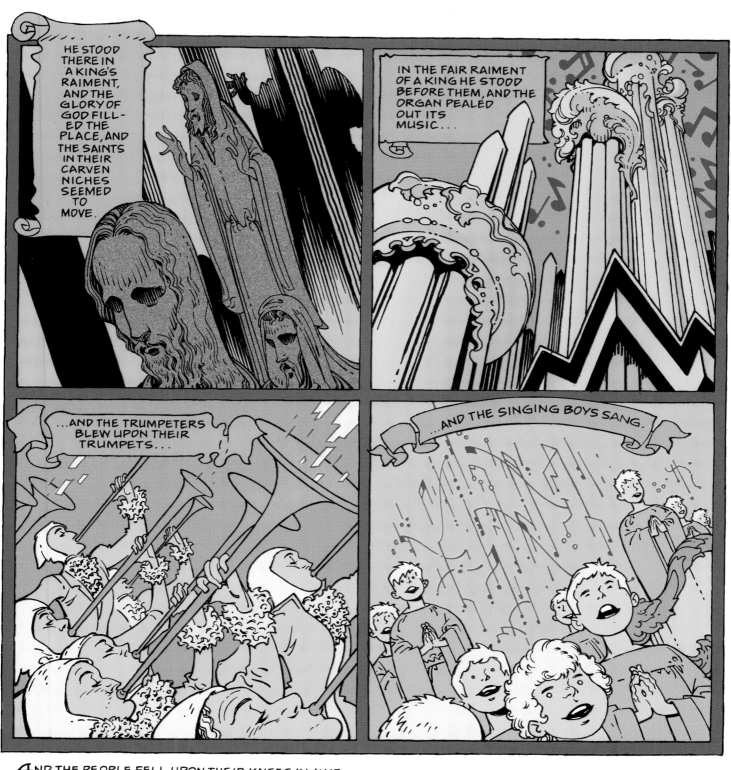

HE STOOD THERE IN A KING'S RAIMENT, AND THE GLORY OF GOD FILLED THE PLACE, AND THE SAINTS IN THEIR CARVEN NICHES SEEMED TO MOVE.

IN THE FAIR RAIMENT OF A KING HE STOOD BEFORE THEM, AND THE ORGAN PEALED OUT ITS MUSIC...

...AND THE TRUMPETERS BLEW UPON THEIR TRUMPETS...

...AND THE SINGING BOYS SANG.

AND THE PEOPLE FELL UPON THEIR KNEES IN AWE...

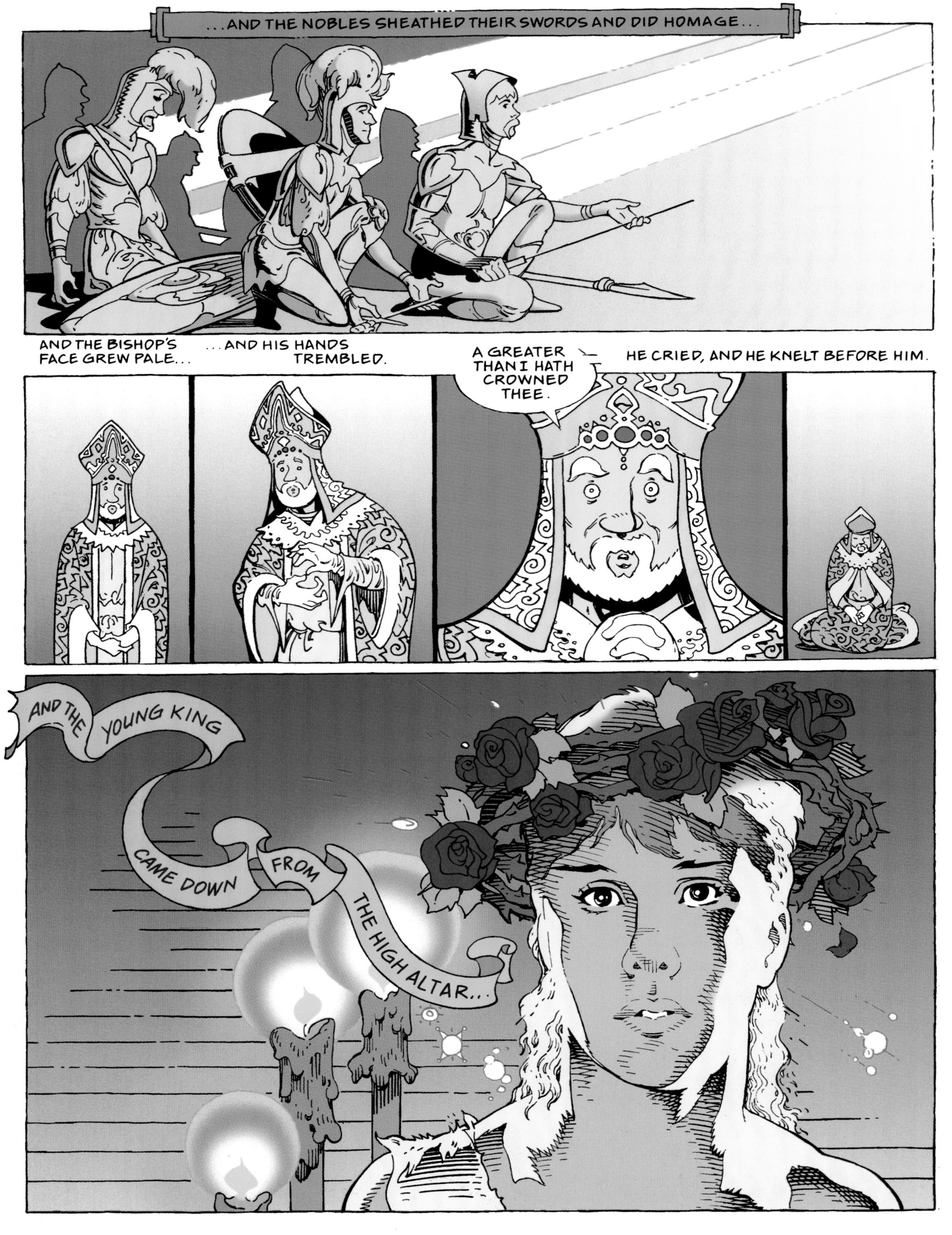
...AND THE NOBLES SHEATHED THEIR SWORDS AND DID HOMAGE...
AND THE BISHOP'S FACE GREW PALE...
...AND HIS HANDS TREMBLED.
A GREATER THAN I HATH CROWNED THEE.
HE CRIED, AND HE KNELT BEFORE HIM.
AND THE YOUNG KING CAME DOWN FROM THE HIGH ALTAR...

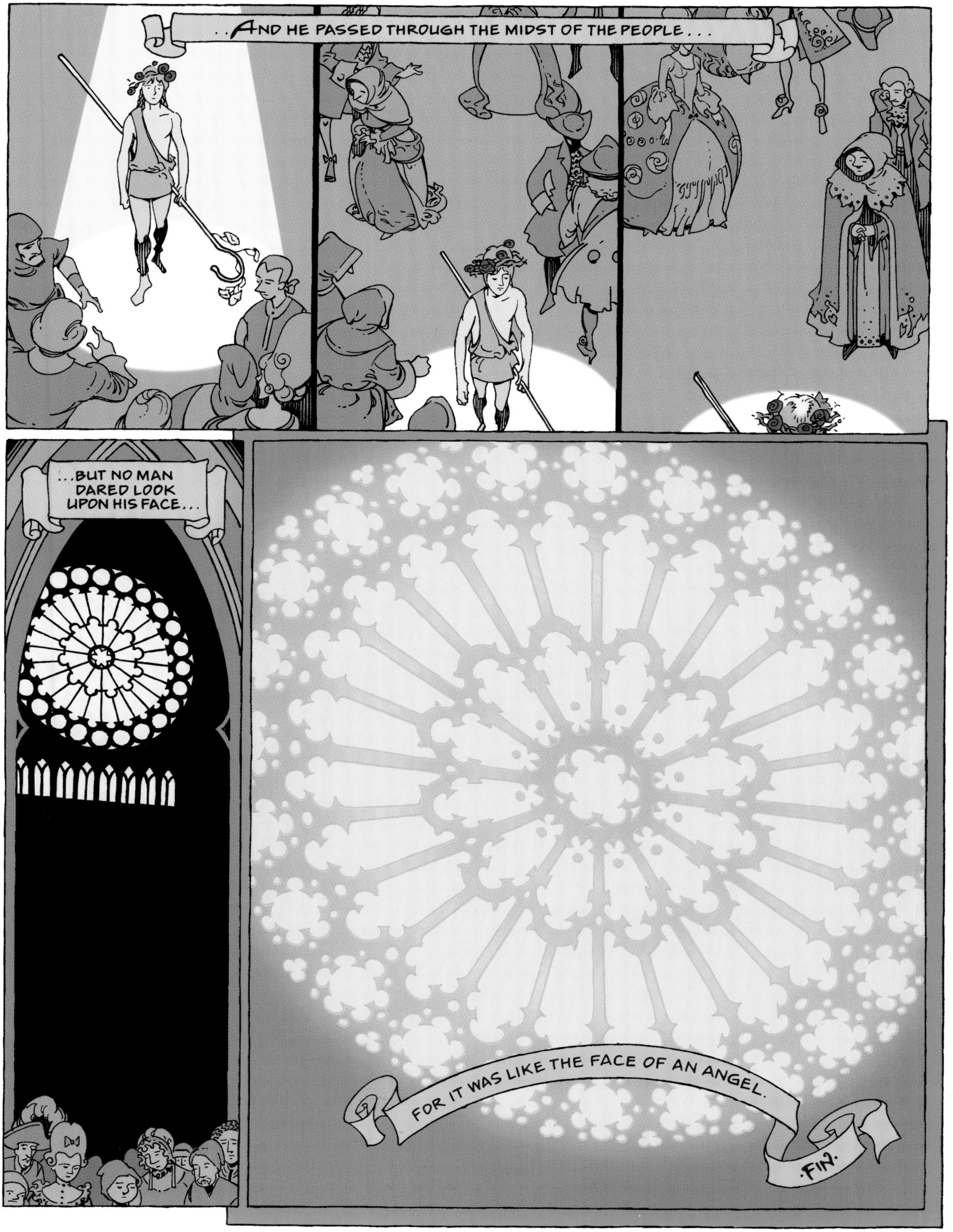
. . . AND HE PASSED THROUGH THE MIDST OF THE PEOPLE . . .
. . . BUT NO MAN DARED LOOK UPON HIS FACE . . .
FOR IT WAS LIKE THE FACE OF AN ANGEL.
FIN.

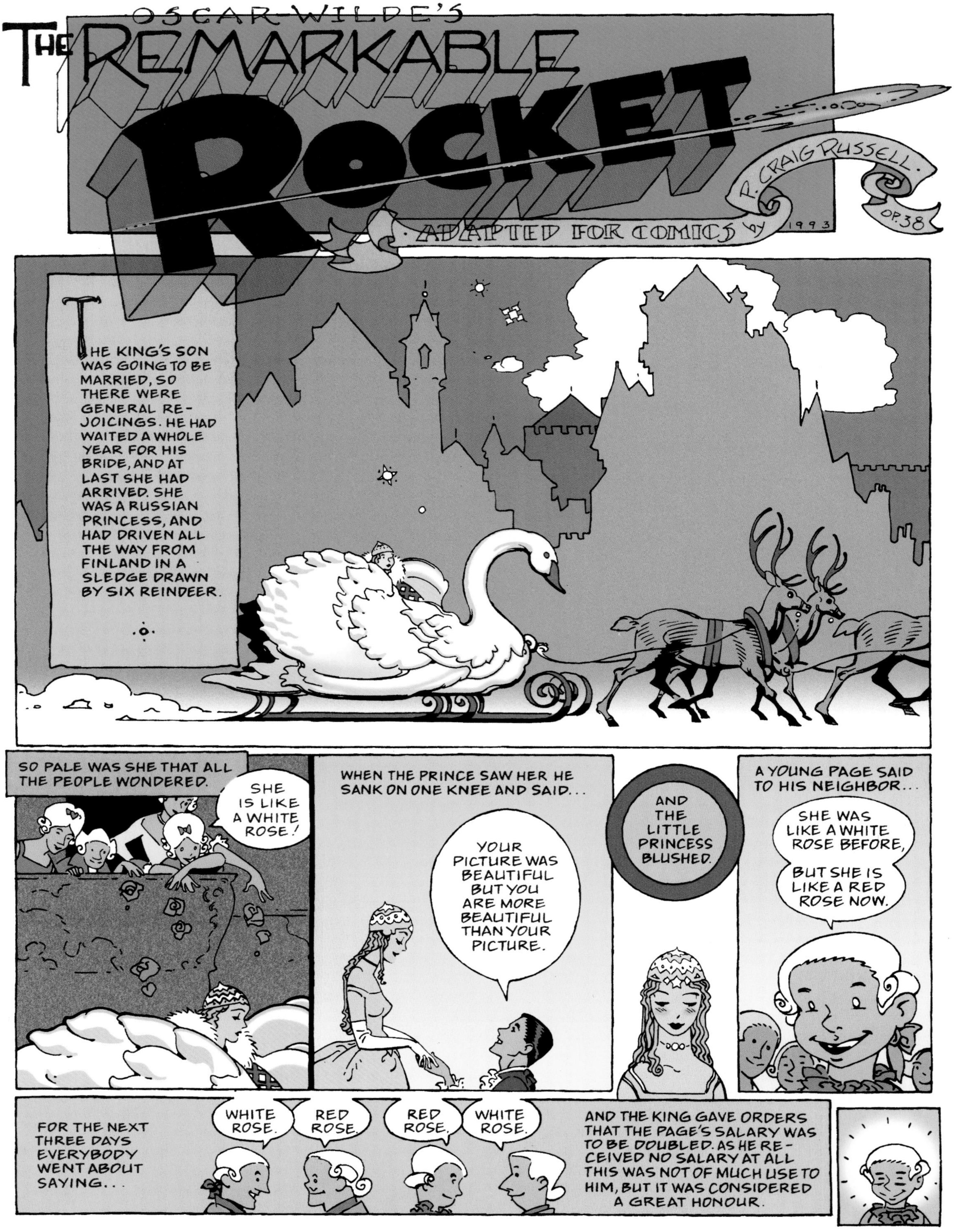
OSCAR WILDE'S
THE REMARKABLE ROCKET
ADAPTED FOR COMICS by P. CRAIG RUSSELL. 1993 OP.38
THE KING'S SON WAS GOING TO BE MARRIED, SO THERE WERE GENERAL RE-JOICINGS. HE HAD WAITED A WHOLE YEAR FOR HIS BRIDE, AND AT LAST SHE HAD ARRIVED. SHE WAS A RUSSIAN PRINCESS, AND HAD DRIVEN ALL THE WAY FROM FINLAND IN A SLEDGE DRAWN BY SIX REINDEER.
SO PALE WAS SHE THAT ALL THE PEOPLE WONDERED.
SHE IS LIKE A WHITE ROSE!
WHEN THE PRINCE SAW HER HE SANK ON ONE KNEE AND SAID...
YOUR PICTURE WAS BEAUTIFUL BUT YOU ARE MORE BEAUTIFUL THAN YOUR PICTURE.
AND THE LITTLE PRINCESS BLUSHED.
A YOUNG PAGE SAID TO HIS NEIGHBOR...
SHE WAS LIKE A WHITE ROSE BEFORE,
BUT SHE IS LIKE A RED ROSE NOW.
FOR THE NEXT THREE DAYS EVERYBODY WENT ABOUT SAYING...
WHITE ROSE.
RED ROSE.
RED ROSE.
WHITE ROSE.
AND THE KING GAVE ORDERS THAT THE PAGE'S SALARY WAS TO BE DOUBLED. AS HE RE-CEIVED NO SALARY AT ALL THIS WAS NOT OF MUCH USE TO HIM, BUT IT WAS CONSIDERED A GREAT HONOUR.

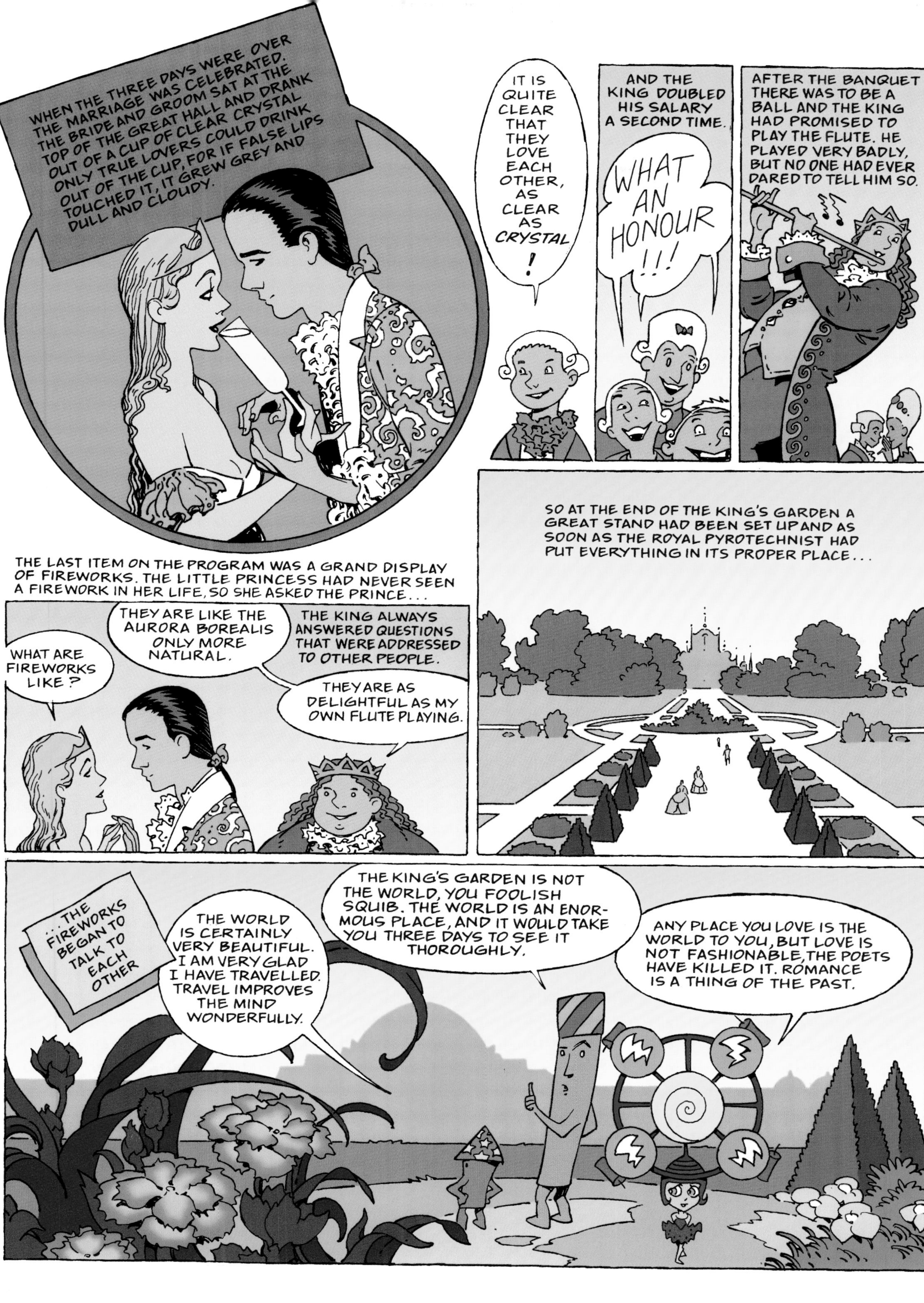
WHEN THE THREE DAYS WERE OVER THE MARRIAGE WAS CELEBRATED. THE BRIDE AND GROOM SAT AT THE TOP OF THE GREAT HALL AND DRANK OUT OF A CUP OF CLEAR CRYSTAL. ONLY TRUE LOVERS COULD DRINK OUT OF THE CUP, FOR IF FALSE LIPS TOUCHED IT, IT GREW GREY AND DULL AND CLOUDY.
IT IS QUITE CLEAR THAT THEY LOVE EACH OTHER, AS CLEAR AS CRYSTAL !
AND THE KING DOUBLED HIS SALARY A SECOND TIME.
WHAT AN HONOUR !!!
AFTER THE BANQUET THERE WAS TO BE A BALL AND THE KING HAD PROMISED TO PLAY THE FLUTE. HE PLAYED VERY BADLY, BUT NO ONE HAD EVER DARED TO TELL HIM SO.
THE LAST ITEM ON THE PROGRAM WAS A GRAND DISPLAY OF FIREWORKS. THE LITTLE PRINCESS HAD NEVER SEEN A FIREWORK IN HER LIFE, SO SHE ASKED THE PRINCE . . .
WHAT ARE FIREWORKS LIKE ?
THEY ARE LIKE THE AURORA BOREALIS ONLY MORE NATURAL.
THE KING ALWAYS ANSWERED QUESTIONS THAT WERE ADDRESSED TO OTHER PEOPLE.
THEY ARE AS DELIGHTFUL AS MY OWN FLUTE PLAYING.
SO AT THE END OF THE KING'S GARDEN A GREAT STAND HAD BEEN SET UP AND AS SOON AS THE ROYAL PYROTECHNIST HAD PUT EVERYTHING IN ITS PROPER PLACE . . .
. . . THE FIREWORKS BEGAN TO TALK TO EACH OTHER
THE WORLD IS CERTAINLY VERY BEAUTIFUL. I AM VERY GLAD I HAVE TRAVELLED. TRAVEL IMPROVES THE MIND WONDERFULLY.
THE KING'S GARDEN IS NOT THE WORLD, YOU FOOLISH SQUIB. THE WORLD IS AN ENORMOUS PLACE, AND IT WOULD TAKE YOU THREE DAYS TO SEE IT THOROUGHLY.
ANY PLACE YOU LOVE IS THE WORLD TO YOU, BUT LOVE IS NOT FASHIONABLE, THE POETS HAVE KILLED IT. ROMANCE IS A THING OF THE PAST.

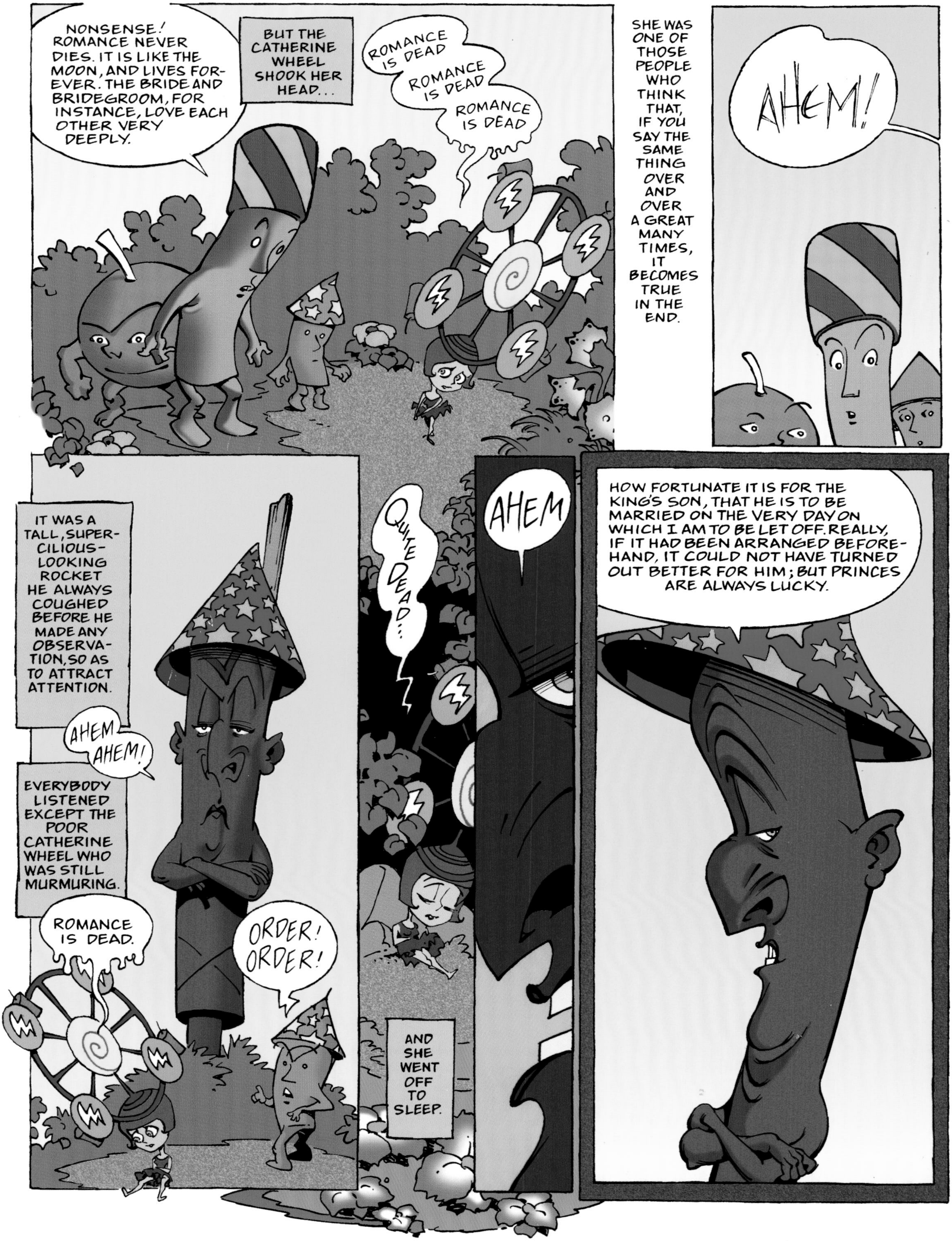
NONSENSE! ROMANCE NEVER DIES. IT IS LIKE THE MOON, AND LIVES FOREVER. THE BRIDE AND BRIDEGROOM, FOR INSTANCE, LOVE EACH OTHER VERY DEEPLY.
BUT THE CATHERINE WHEEL SHOOK HER HEAD...
ROMANCE IS DEAD
ROMANCE IS DEAD
ROMANCE IS DEAD
SHE WAS ONE OF THOSE PEOPLE WHO THINK THAT, IF YOU SAY THE SAME THING OVER AND OVER A GREAT MANY TIMES, IT BECOMES TRUE IN THE END.
AHEM!
IT WAS A TALL, SUPERCILIOUS-LOOKING ROCKET HE ALWAYS COUGHED BEFORE HE MADE ANY OBSERVATION, SO AS TO ATTRACT ATTENTION.
AHEM AHEM!
EVERYBODY LISTENED EXCEPT THE POOR CATHERINE WHEEL WHO WAS STILL MURMURING.
ROMANCE IS DEAD.
ORDER! ORDER!
QUITE DEAD...
AND SHE WENT OFF TO SLEEP.
AHEM
HOW FORTUNATE IT IS FOR THE KING'S SON, THAT HE IS TO BE MARRIED ON THE VERY DAY ON WHICH I AM TO BE LET OFF. REALLY, IF IT HAD BEEN ARRANGED BEFOREHAND, IT COULD NOT HAVE TURNED OUT BETTER FOR HIM; BUT PRINCES ARE ALWAYS LUCKY.

DEAR ME! I THOUGHT IT WAS QUITE THE OTHER WAY, AND THAT WE WERE TO BE LET OFF IN THE PRINCE'S HONOUR.

IT MAY BE SO WITH YOU, BUT WITH ME IT IS DIFFERENT. I AM A VERY REMARKABLE ROCKET AND COME OF REMARKABLE PARENTS.

"MY MOTHER WAS THE MOST CELEBRATED CATHERINE WHEEL OF HER DAY, AND WAS RENOWNED FOR HER GRACEFUL DANCING."

"MY FATHER WAS A ROCKET LIKE MYSELF, AND OF FRENCH EXTRACTION. HE FLEW REMARKABLY HIGH AND MADE A MOST BRILLIANT DESCENT IN A SHOWER OF GOLDEN RAIN. THE NEWSPAPERS CALLED HIM A TRIUMPH OF *PYLOTECHNIC* ART."

PYRO-TECHNIC, PYRO-TECHNIC, YOU MEAN. I KNOW IT IS PYROTECHNIC, FOR I SAW IT WRITTEN ON MY OWN CANISTER.

WELL *I* SAID *PYLOTECHNIC!*

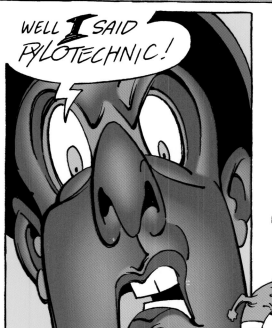

THE BENGAL LIGHT FELT SO CRUSHED THAT HE BEGAN AT ONCE TO BULLY THE LITTLE SQUIBS IN ORDER TO SHOW THAT HE WAS STILL A PERSON OF SOME IMPORTANCE.

I WAS SAYING, I WAS SAYING,

WHAT WAS I SAYING?

YOU WERE TALKING ABOUT YOURSELF.

OF COURSE; I KNEW I WAS DISCUSSING SOME INTERESTING SUBJECT WHEN I WAS SO RUDELY INTERRUPTED. I HATE RUDENESS AND BAD MANNERS, FOR I AM EXTREMELY SENSITIVE.

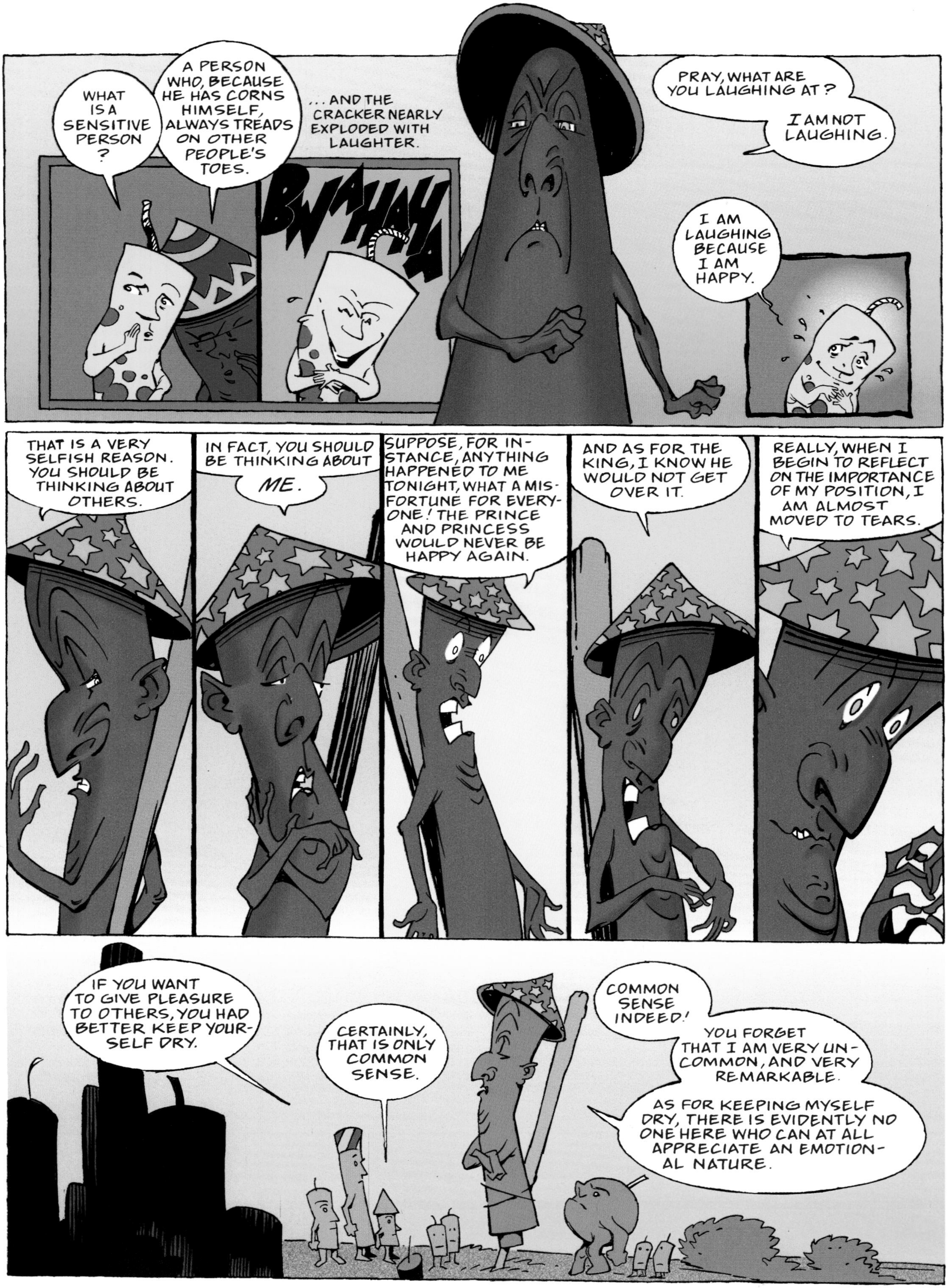
WHAT IS A SENSITIVE PERSON ?
A PERSON WHO, BECAUSE HE HAS CORNS HIMSELF, ALWAYS TREADS ON OTHER PEOPLE'S TOES.
. . . AND THE CRACKER NEARLY EXPLODED WITH LAUGHTER.
BWAHAHAHA
PRAY, WHAT ARE YOU LAUGHING AT ?
I AM NOT LAUGHING.
I AM LAUGHING BECAUSE I AM HAPPY.
THAT IS A VERY SELFISH REASON. YOU SHOULD BE THINKING ABOUT OTHERS.
IN FACT, YOU SHOULD BE THINKING ABOUT ME.
SUPPOSE, FOR INSTANCE, ANYTHING HAPPENED TO ME TONIGHT, WHAT A MISFORTUNE FOR EVERYONE! THE PRINCE AND PRINCESS WOULD NEVER BE HAPPY AGAIN.
AND AS FOR THE KING, I KNOW HE WOULD NOT GET OVER IT.
REALLY, WHEN I BEGIN TO REFLECT ON THE IMPORTANCE OF MY POSITION, I AM ALMOST MOVED TO TEARS.
IF YOU WANT TO GIVE PLEASURE TO OTHERS, YOU HAD BETTER KEEP YOURSELF DRY.
CERTAINLY, THAT IS ONLY COMMON SENSE.
COMMON SENSE INDEED!
YOU FORGET THAT I AM VERY UNCOMMON, AND VERY REMARKABLE.
AS FOR KEEPING MYSELF DRY, THERE IS EVIDENTLY NO ONE HERE WHO CAN AT ALL APPRECIATE AN EMOTIONAL NATURE.

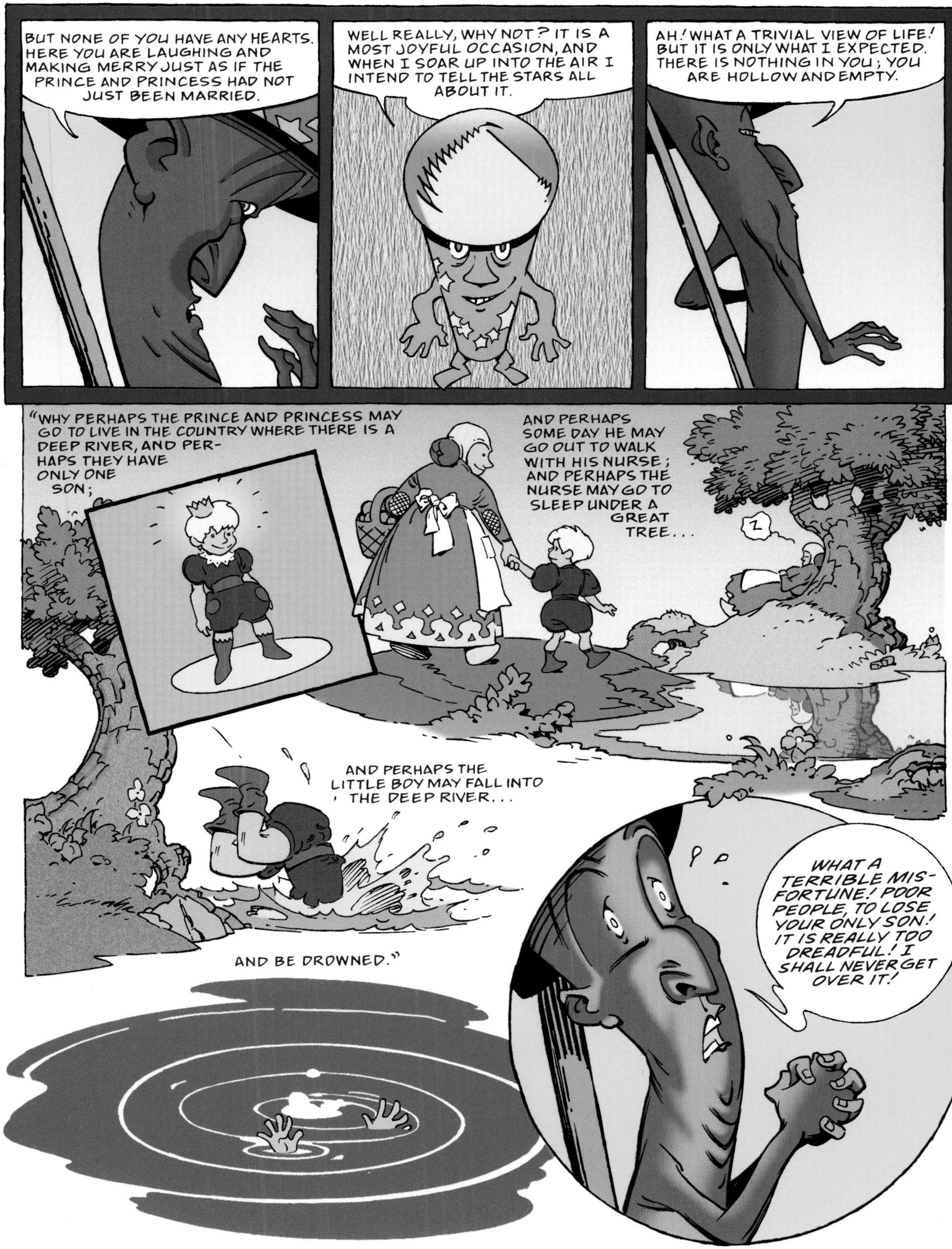
BUT NONE OF YOU HAVE ANY HEARTS. HERE YOU ARE LAUGHING AND MAKING MERRY JUST AS IF THE PRINCE AND PRINCESS HAD NOT JUST BEEN MARRIED.
WELL REALLY, WHY NOT? IT IS A MOST JOYFUL OCCASION, AND WHEN I SOAR UP INTO THE AIR I INTEND TO TELL THE STARS ALL ABOUT IT.
AH! WHAT A TRIVIAL VIEW OF LIFE! BUT IT IS ONLY WHAT I EXPECTED. THERE IS NOTHING IN YOU; YOU ARE HOLLOW AND EMPTY.
"WHY PERHAPS THE PRINCE AND PRINCESS MAY GO TO LIVE IN THE COUNTRY WHERE THERE IS A DEEP RIVER, AND PERHAPS THEY HAVE ONLY ONE SON;
AND PERHAPS SOME DAY HE MAY GO OUT TO WALK WITH HIS NURSE; AND PERHAPS THE NURSE MAY GO TO SLEEP UNDER A GREAT TREE...
Z
AND PERHAPS THE LITTLE BOY MAY FALL INTO THE DEEP RIVER...
AND BE DROWNED."
WHAT A TERRIBLE MISFORTUNE! POOR PEOPLE, TO LOSE YOUR ONLY SON! IT IS REALLY TOO DREADFUL! I SHALL NEVER GET OVER IT!

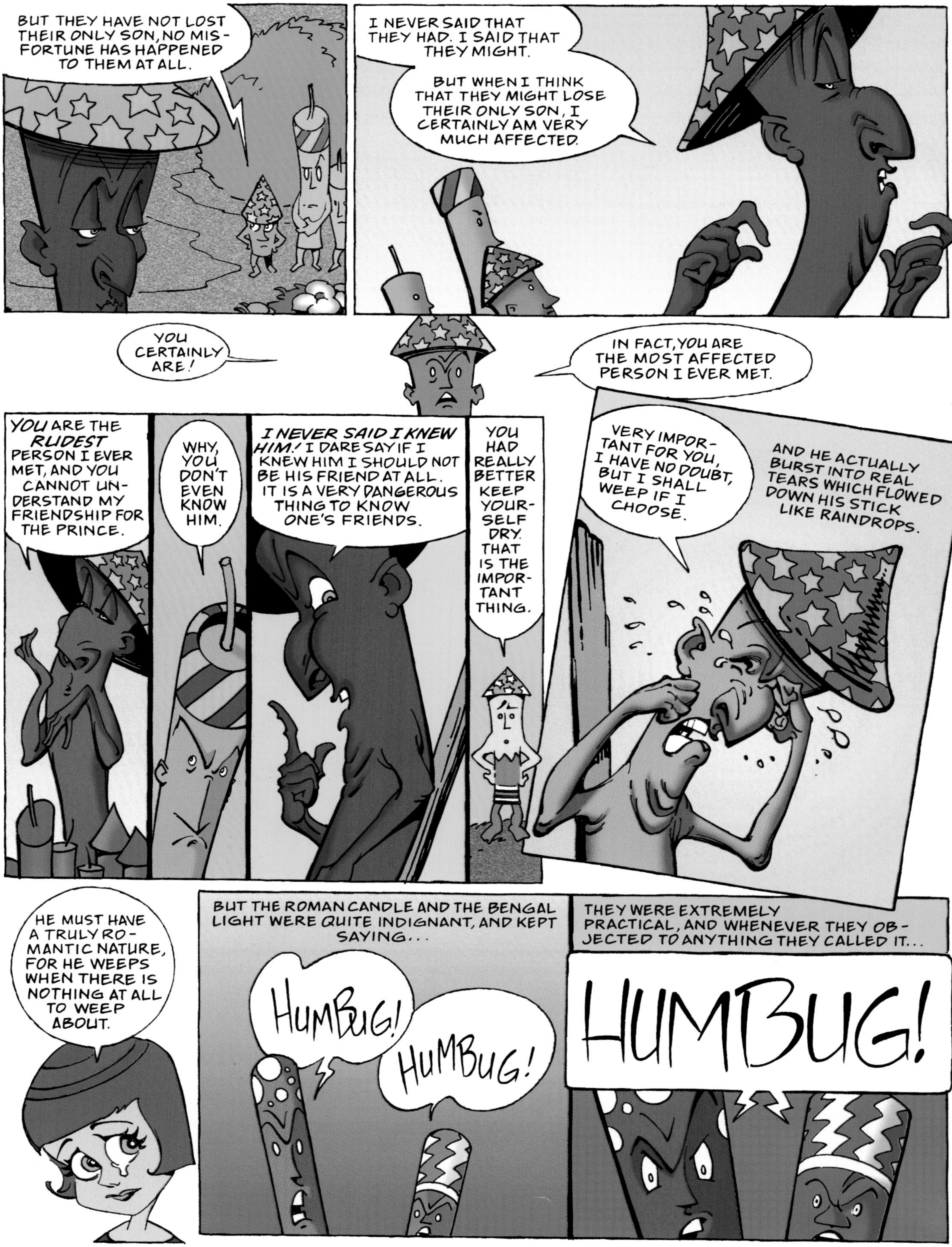
BUT THEY HAVE NOT LOST THEIR ONLY SON, NO MISFORTUNE HAS HAPPENED TO THEM AT ALL.
I NEVER SAID THAT THEY HAD. I SAID THAT THEY MIGHT.
BUT WHEN I THINK THAT THEY MIGHT LOSE THEIR ONLY SON, I CERTAINLY AM VERY MUCH AFFECTED.
YOU CERTAINLY ARE!
IN FACT, YOU ARE THE MOST AFFECTED PERSON I EVER MET.
YOU ARE THE RUDEST PERSON I EVER MET, AND YOU CANNOT UNDERSTAND MY FRIENDSHIP FOR THE PRINCE.
WHY, YOU DON'T EVEN KNOW HIM.
I NEVER SAID I KNEW HIM! I DARE SAY IF I KNEW HIM I SHOULD NOT BE HIS FRIEND AT ALL. IT IS A VERY DANGEROUS THING TO KNOW ONE'S FRIENDS.
YOU HAD REALLY BETTER KEEP YOURSELF DRY. THAT IS THE IMPORTANT THING.
VERY IMPORTANT FOR YOU, I HAVE NO DOUBT, BUT I SHALL WEEP IF I CHOOSE.
AND HE ACTUALLY BURST INTO REAL TEARS WHICH FLOWED DOWN HIS STICK LIKE RAINDROPS.
HE MUST HAVE A TRULY ROMANTIC NATURE, FOR HE WEEPS WHEN THERE IS NOTHING AT ALL TO WEEP ABOUT.
BUT THE ROMAN CANDLE AND THE BENGAL LIGHT WERE QUITE INDIGNANT, AND KEPT SAYING...
HUMBUG!
HUMBUG!
THEY WERE EXTREMELY PRACTICAL, AND WHENEVER THEY OBJECTED TO ANYTHING THEY CALLED IT...
HUMBUG!

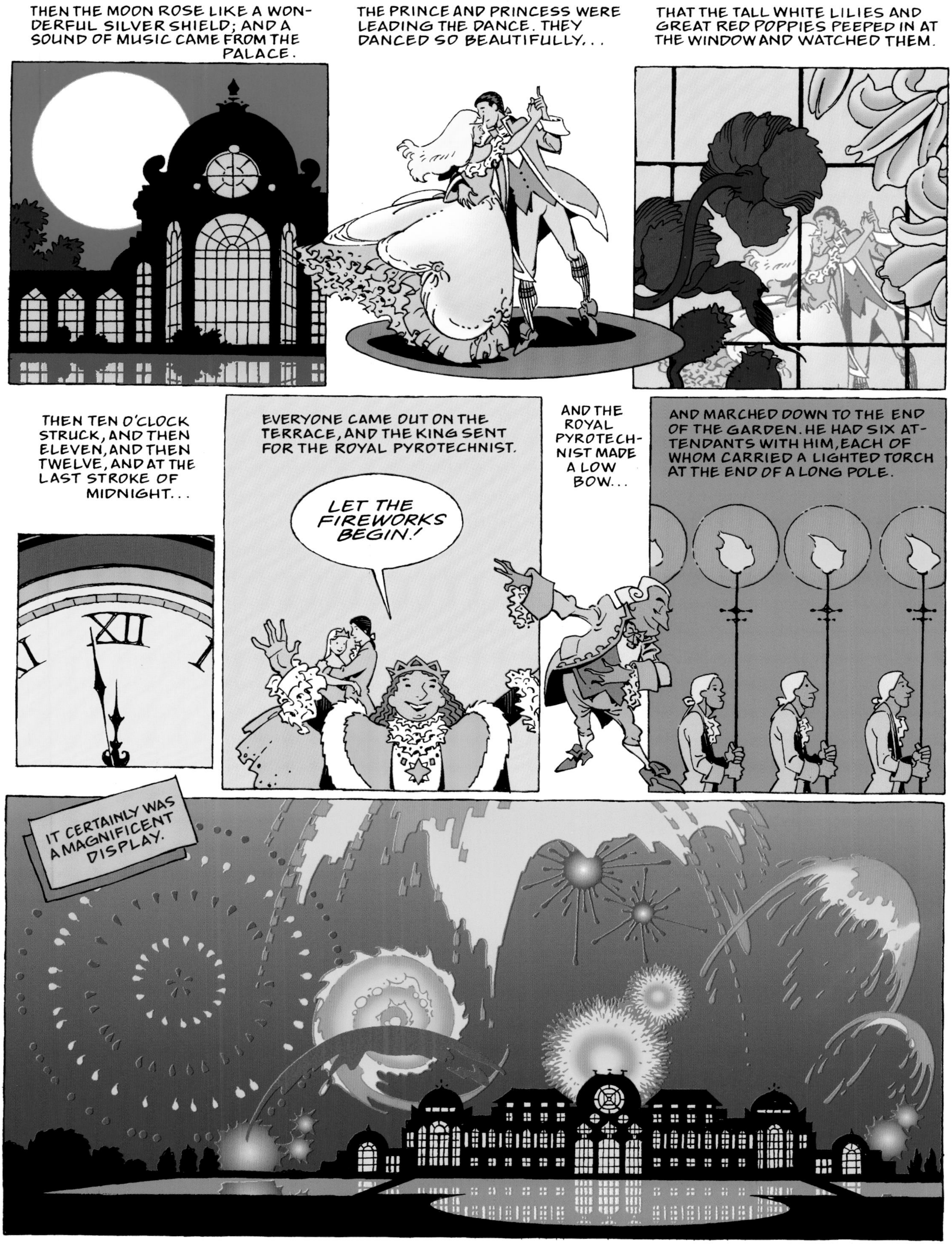

THEN THE MOON ROSE LIKE A WONDERFUL SILVER SHIELD; AND A SOUND OF MUSIC CAME FROM THE PALACE.
THE PRINCE AND PRINCESS WERE LEADING THE DANCE. THEY DANCED SO BEAUTIFULLY...
THAT THE TALL WHITE LILIES AND GREAT RED POPPIES PEEPED IN AT THE WINDOW AND WATCHED THEM.
THEN TEN O'CLOCK STRUCK, AND THEN ELEVEN, AND THEN TWELVE, AND AT THE LAST STROKE OF MIDNIGHT...
XII
EVERYONE CAME OUT ON THE TERRACE, AND THE KING SENT FOR THE ROYAL PYROTECHNIST.
LET THE FIREWORKS BEGIN!
AND THE ROYAL PYROTECHNIST MADE A LOW BOW...
AND MARCHED DOWN TO THE END OF THE GARDEN. HE HAD SIX ATTENDANTS WITH HIM, EACH OF WHOM CARRIED A LIGHTED TORCH AT THE END OF A LONG POLE.
IT CERTAINLY WAS A MAGNIFICENT DISPLAY.

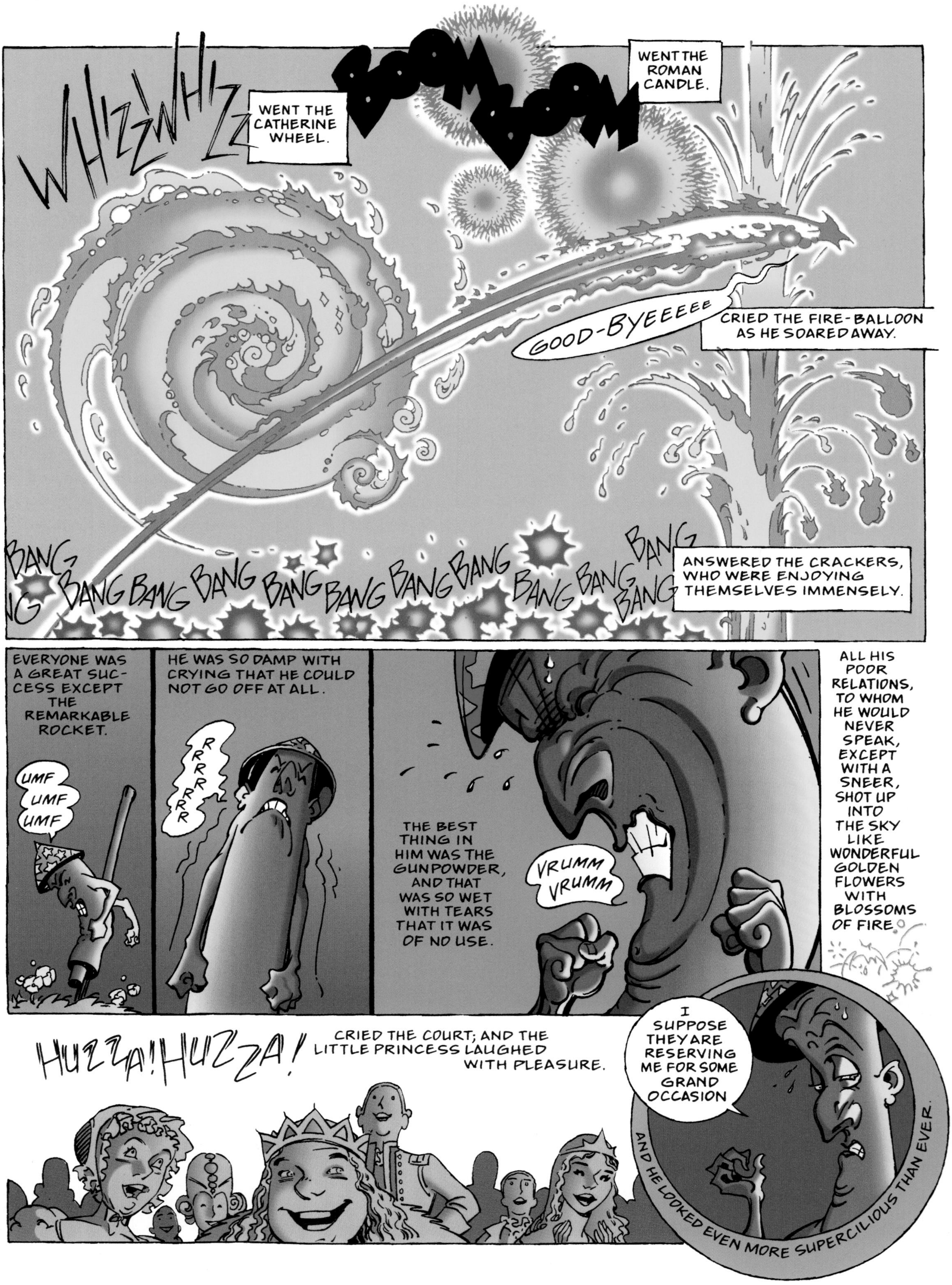
WHIZZ WHIZZ
WENT THE CATHERINE WHEEL.
BOOM BOOM
WENT THE ROMAN CANDLE.
GOOD-BYEEEEE
CRIED THE FIRE-BALLOON AS HE SOARED AWAY.
BANG BANG BANG BANG BANG BANG BANG BANG BANG BANG BANG BANG BANG
ANSWERED THE CRACKERS, WHO WERE ENJOYING THEMSELVES IMMENSELY.
EVERYONE WAS A GREAT SUCCESS EXCEPT THE REMARKABLE ROCKET.
UMF UMF UMF
HE WAS SO DAMP WITH CRYING THAT HE COULD NOT GO OFF AT ALL.
RRRRRR
THE BEST THING IN HIM WAS THE GUNPOWDER, AND THAT WAS SO WET WITH TEARS THAT IT WAS OF NO USE.
VRUMM VRUMM
ALL HIS POOR RELATIONS, TO WHOM HE WOULD NEVER SPEAK, EXCEPT WITH A SNEER, SHOT UP INTO THE SKY LIKE WONDERFUL GOLDEN FLOWERS WITH BLOSSOMS OF FIRE.
HUZZA! HUZZA!
CRIED THE COURT; AND THE LITTLE PRINCESS LAUGHED WITH PLEASURE.
I SUPPOSE THEY ARE RESERVING ME FOR SOME GRAND OCCASION
AND HE LOOKED EVEN MORE SUPERCILIOUS THAN EVER.

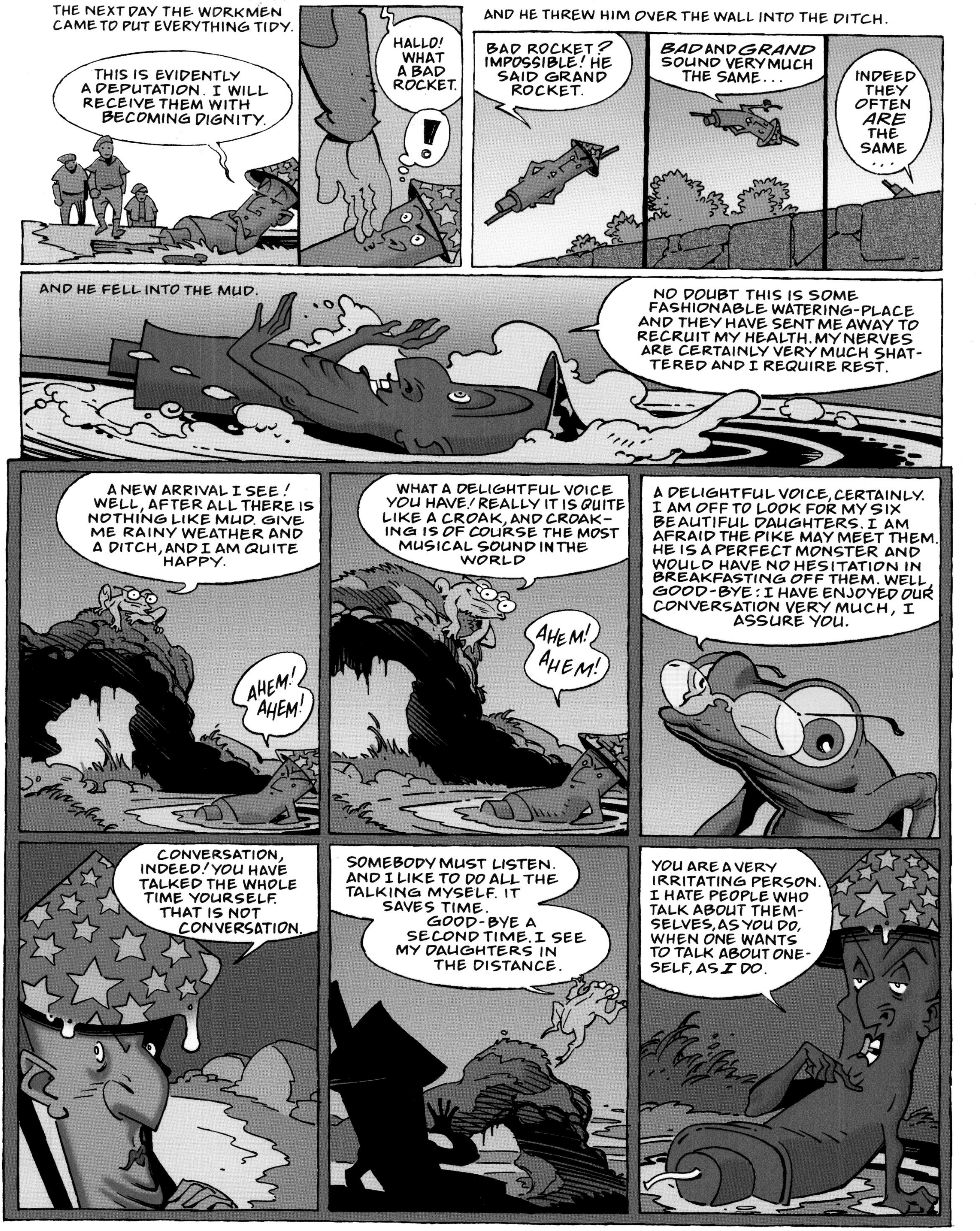
THE NEXT DAY THE WORKMEN CAME TO PUT EVERYTHING TIDY.
THIS IS EVIDENTLY A DEPUTATION. I WILL RECEIVE THEM WITH BECOMING DIGNITY.
HALLO! WHAT A BAD ROCKET.
!
AND HE THREW HIM OVER THE WALL INTO THE DITCH.
BAD ROCKET? IMPOSSIBLE! HE SAID GRAND ROCKET.
BAD AND GRAND SOUND VERY MUCH THE SAME...
INDEED THEY OFTEN ARE THE SAME...
AND HE FELL INTO THE MUD.
NO DOUBT THIS IS SOME FASHIONABLE WATERING-PLACE AND THEY HAVE SENT ME AWAY TO RECRUIT MY HEALTH. MY NERVES ARE CERTAINLY VERY MUCH SHATTERED AND I REQUIRE REST.
A NEW ARRIVAL I SEE! WELL, AFTER ALL THERE IS NOTHING LIKE MUD. GIVE ME RAINY WEATHER AND A DITCH, AND I AM QUITE HAPPY.
AHEM! AHEM!
WHAT A DELIGHTFUL VOICE YOU HAVE! REALLY IT IS QUITE LIKE A CROAK, AND CROAKING IS OF COURSE THE MOST MUSICAL SOUND IN THE WORLD
AHEM! AHEM!
A DELIGHTFUL VOICE, CERTAINLY. I AM OFF TO LOOK FOR MY SIX BEAUTIFUL DAUGHTERS. I AM AFRAID THE PIKE MAY MEET THEM. HE IS A PERFECT MONSTER AND WOULD HAVE NO HESITATION IN BREAKFASTING OFF THEM. WELL GOOD-BYE: I HAVE ENJOYED OUR CONVERSATION VERY MUCH, I ASSURE YOU.
CONVERSATION, INDEED! YOU HAVE TALKED THE WHOLE TIME YOURSELF. THAT IS NOT CONVERSATION.
SOMEBODY MUST LISTEN. AND I LIKE TO DO ALL THE TALKING MYSELF. IT SAVES TIME.
GOOD-BYE A SECOND TIME. I SEE MY DAUGHTERS IN THE DISTANCE.
YOU ARE A VERY IRRITATING PERSON. I HATE PEOPLE WHO TALK ABOUT THEMSELVES, AS YOU DO, WHEN ONE WANTS TO TALK ABOUT ONESELF, AS I DO.

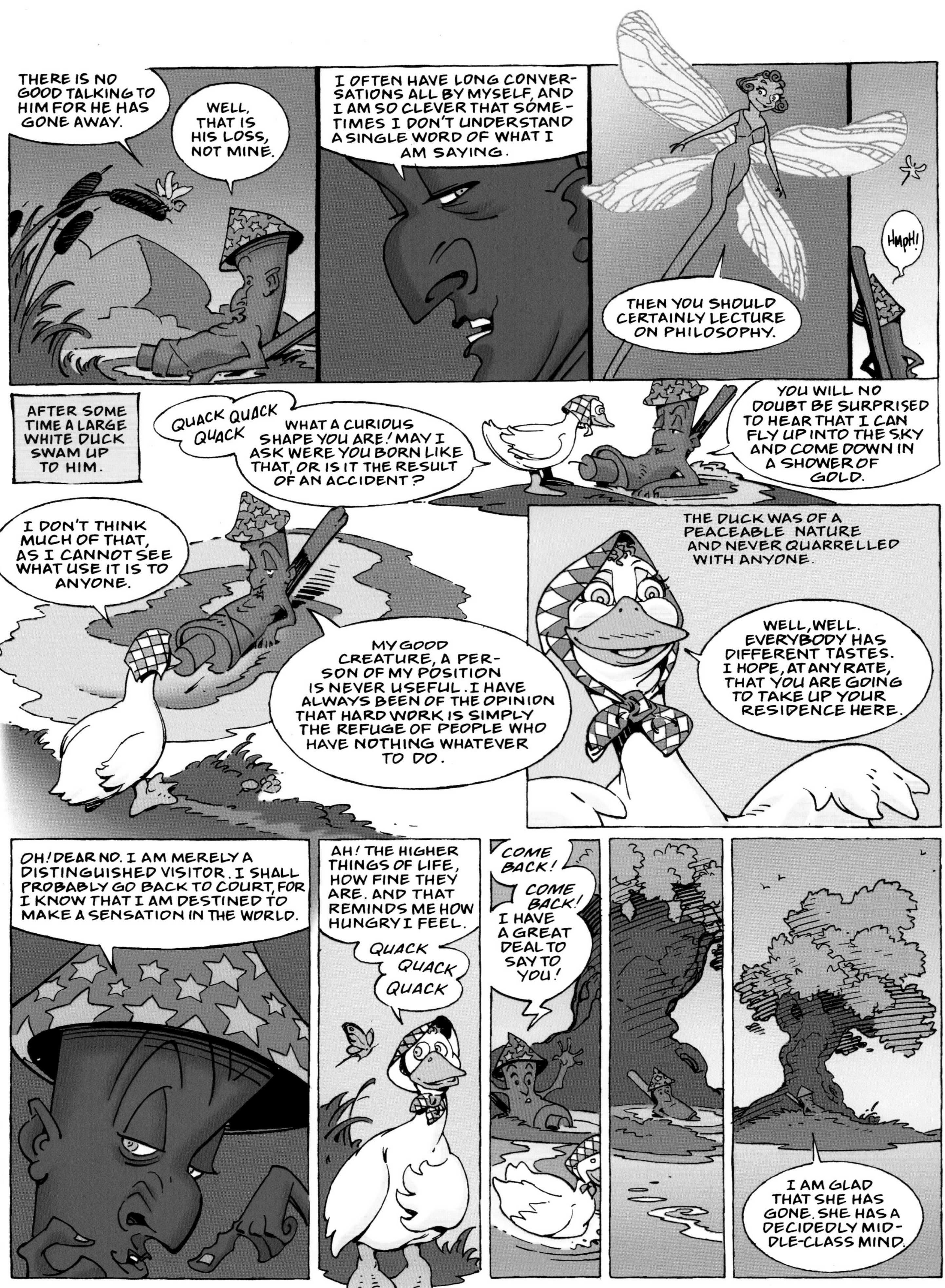
THERE IS NO GOOD TALKING TO HIM FOR HE HAS GONE AWAY.
WELL, THAT IS HIS LOSS, NOT MINE.
I OFTEN HAVE LONG CONVERSATIONS ALL BY MYSELF, AND I AM SO CLEVER THAT SOMETIMES I DON'T UNDERSTAND A SINGLE WORD OF WHAT I AM SAYING.
THEN YOU SHOULD CERTAINLY LECTURE ON PHILOSOPHY.
HMPH!
AFTER SOME TIME A LARGE WHITE DUCK SWAM UP TO HIM.
QUACK QUACK QUACK
WHAT A CURIOUS SHAPE YOU ARE! MAY I ASK WERE YOU BORN LIKE THAT, OR IS IT THE RESULT OF AN ACCIDENT?
YOU WILL NO DOUBT BE SURPRISED TO HEAR THAT I CAN FLY UP INTO THE SKY AND COME DOWN IN A SHOWER OF GOLD.
I DON'T THINK MUCH OF THAT, AS I CANNOT SEE WHAT USE IT IS TO ANYONE.
MY GOOD CREATURE, A PERSON OF MY POSITION IS NEVER USEFUL. I HAVE ALWAYS BEEN OF THE OPINION THAT HARD WORK IS SIMPLY THE REFUGE OF PEOPLE WHO HAVE NOTHING WHATEVER TO DO.
THE DUCK WAS OF A PEACEABLE NATURE AND NEVER QUARRELLED WITH ANYONE.
WELL, WELL. EVERYBODY HAS DIFFERENT TASTES. I HOPE, AT ANY RATE, THAT YOU ARE GOING TO TAKE UP YOUR RESIDENCE HERE.
OH! DEAR NO. I AM MERELY A DISTINGUISHED VISITOR. I SHALL PROBABLY GO BACK TO COURT, FOR I KNOW THAT I AM DESTINED TO MAKE A SENSATION IN THE WORLD.
AH! THE HIGHER THINGS OF LIFE, HOW FINE THEY ARE. AND THAT REMINDS ME HOW HUNGRY I FEEL.
QUACK QUACK QUACK
COME BACK!
COME BACK! I HAVE A GREAT DEAL TO SAY TO YOU!
I AM GLAD THAT SHE HAS GONE. SHE HAS A DECIDEDLY MIDDLE-CLASS MIND.

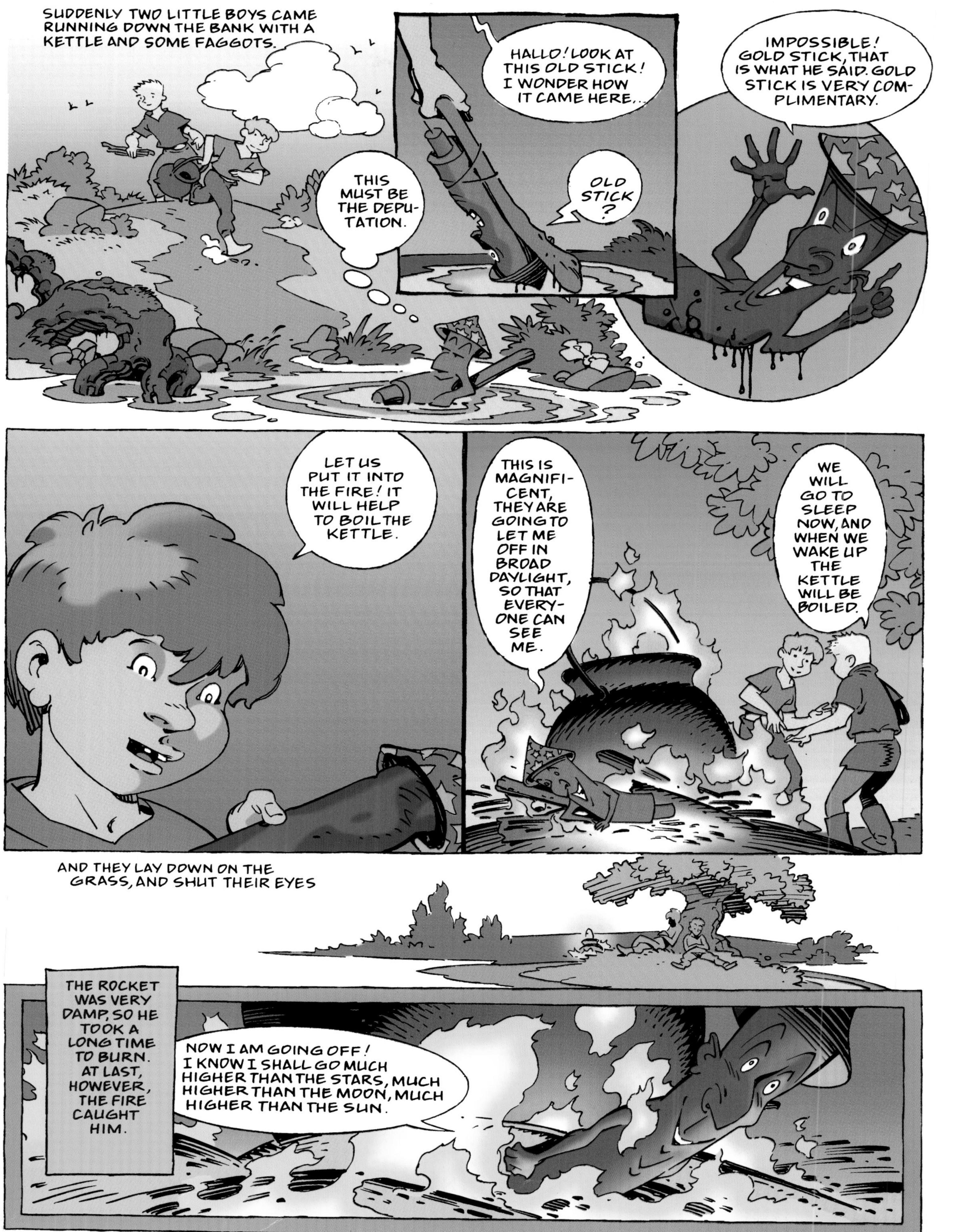
SUDDENLY TWO LITTLE BOYS CAME RUNNING DOWN THE BANK WITH A KETTLE AND SOME FAGGOTS.
THIS MUST BE THE DEPUTATION.
HALLO! LOOK AT THIS OLD STICK! I WONDER HOW IT CAME HERE...
OLD STICK?
IMPOSSIBLE! GOLD STICK, THAT IS WHAT HE SAID. GOLD STICK IS VERY COMPLIMENTARY.
LET US PUT IT INTO THE FIRE! IT WILL HELP TO BOIL THE KETTLE.
THIS IS MAGNIFICENT, THEY ARE GOING TO LET ME OFF IN BROAD DAYLIGHT, SO THAT EVERYONE CAN SEE ME.
WE WILL GO TO SLEEP NOW, AND WHEN WE WAKE UP THE KETTLE WILL BE BOILED.
AND THEY LAY DOWN ON THE GRASS, AND SHUT THEIR EYES
THE ROCKET WAS VERY DAMP, SO HE TOOK A LONG TIME TO BURN. AT LAST, HOWEVER, THE FIRE CAUGHT HIM.
NOW I AM GOING OFF! I KNOW I SHALL GO MUCH HIGHER THAN THE STARS, MUCH HIGHER THAN THE MOON, MUCH HIGHER THAN THE SUN.

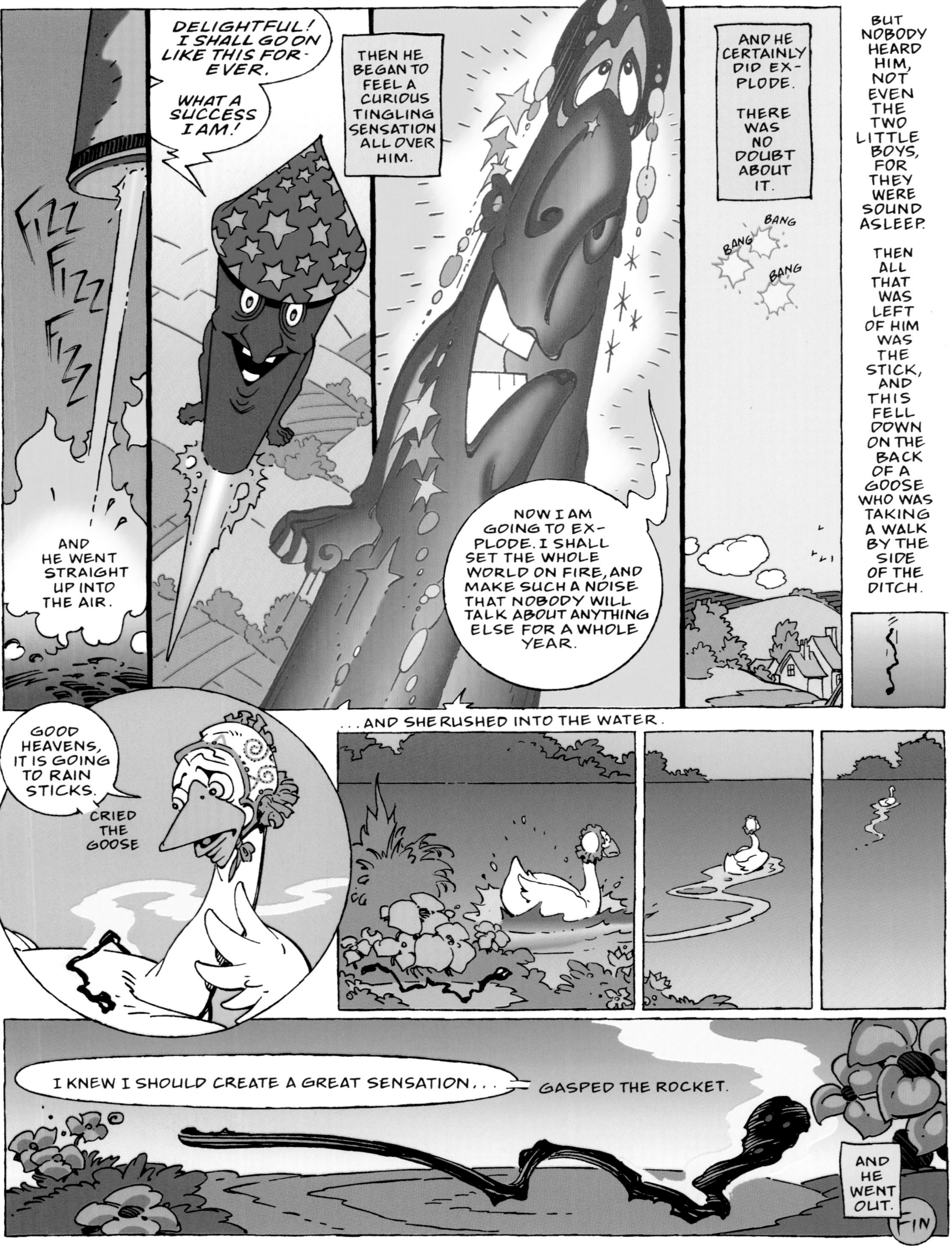
FIZZ FIZZ FIZZ
AND HE WENT STRAIGHT UP INTO THE AIR.
DELIGHTFUL! I SHALL GO ON LIKE THIS FOR-EVER.
WHAT A SUCCESS I AM!
THEN HE BEGAN TO FEEL A CURIOUS TINGLING SENSATION ALL OVER HIM.
NOW I AM GOING TO EX-PLODE. I SHALL SET THE WHOLE WORLD ON FIRE, AND MAKE SUCH A NOISE THAT NOBODY WILL TALK ABOUT ANYTHING ELSE FOR A WHOLE YEAR.
AND HE CERTAINLY DID EX-PLODE.
THERE WAS NO DOUBT ABOUT IT.
BANG
BANG
BANG
BUT NOBODY HEARD HIM, NOT EVEN THE TWO LITTLE BOYS, FOR THEY WERE SOUND ASLEEP.
THEN ALL THAT WAS LEFT OF HIM WAS THE STICK, AND THIS FELL DOWN ON THE BACK OF A GOOSE WHO WAS TAKING A WALK BY THE SIDE OF THE DITCH.
GOOD HEAVENS, IT IS GOING TO RAIN STICKS.
CRIED THE GOOSE
. . . AND SHE RUSHED INTO THE WATER .
I KNEW I SHOULD CREATE A GREAT SENSATION . . .
GASPED THE ROCKET.
AND HE WENT OUT.
FIN

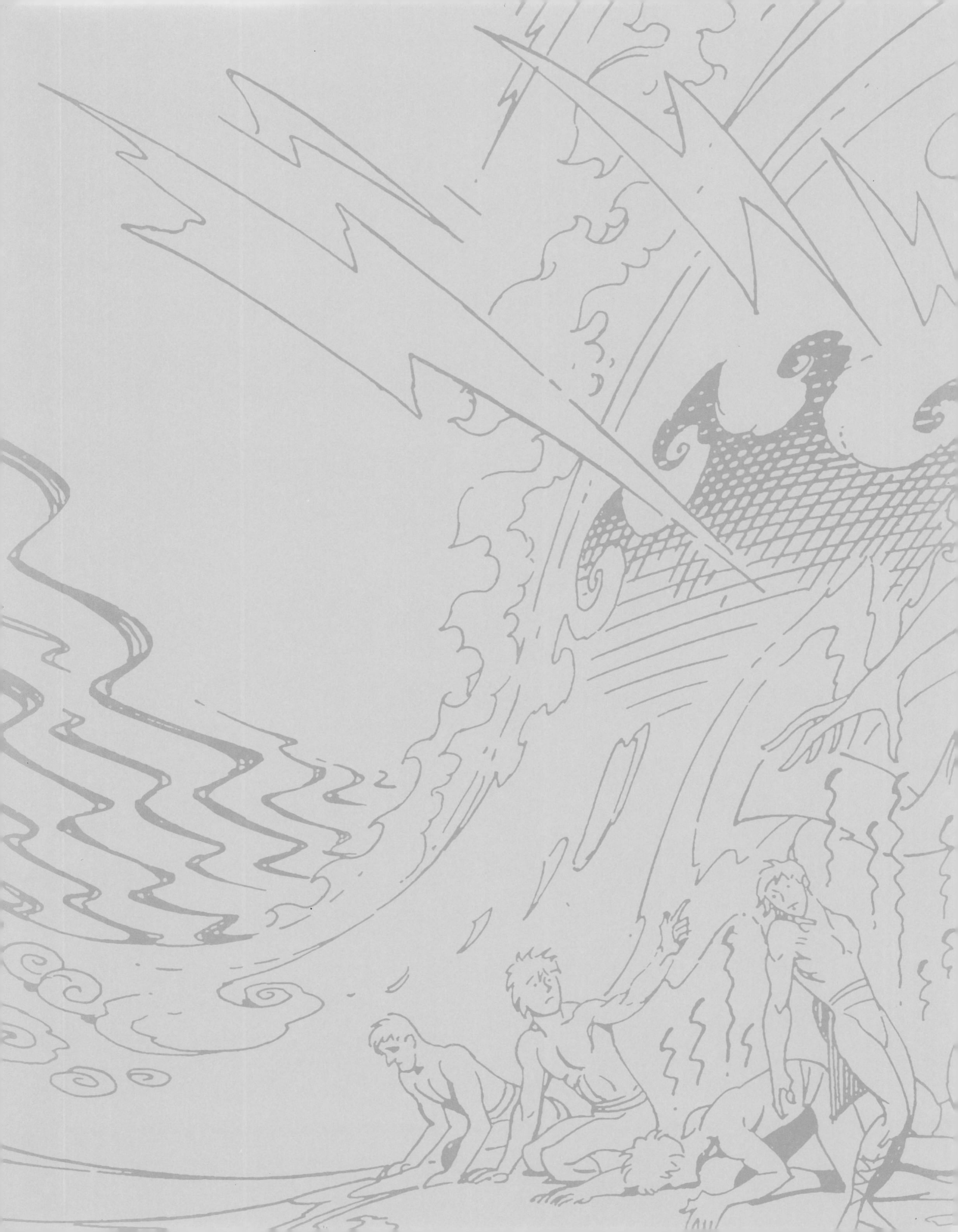